THE UNKINDEST CUT

They were standing close together, very close, and Karnobat brought up a sudden knee, very hard, into Cass's groin, and Cass stepped back and twisted sideways, and struck at it with an aluminum leg—a hard, sharp, and deadly blow—and the Captain went sprawling in the wet earth, lying there and looking up in shocked surprise.

The long hunting knife was already in his hand when he leaped up, grimacing at the pain of a cracked kneecap, and he stood in a crouch and waited. Cass smiled and said, "Are you coming at me, or shall I come at you? It's all the same, Captain."

The men around the fire had gotten to their feet and were forming a circle round them, and one of them said, jeering, "You don't need the knife, Karnobat, he's old enough to be your grandfather."

He did not take his eyes off Cass. He said slowly: "Oh, I'm not going to hurt him, the Major wants to see him in the morning. I'm just going to cut his ears off, make him hear good . . ."

TOBIN'S WAR SERIES:

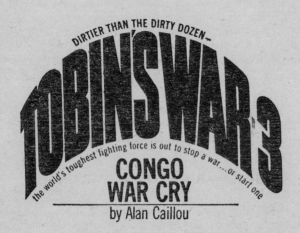

DIRTIER THAN THE DIRTY DOZEN—

TOBIN'S WAR 3

the world's toughest fighting force is out to stop a war...or start one

CONGO WAR CRY

by Alan Caillou

PINNACLE BOOKS   LOS ANGELES

TOBIN'S WAR #3: CONGO WAR CRY

Copyright © 1972 by Alan Caillou

An original Pinnacle Books edition, published
for the first time anywhere.

First printing, January 1972
Second printing, October 1980

ISBN: 0-523-41029-8

Cover illustration by Bruce Minney

Printed in the United States of America

PINNACLE BOOKS, INC.
2029 Century Park East
Los Angeles, California 90067

Congo War Cry

CHAPTER ONE

CONGO
CO-ORDINATES: 21.18E
07.17S

The air line had taken them as far as Moanda, on the broad estuary of the Congo River, nearly three thousand miles of black and muddy waters draining an area of a million and a half square miles. Here, they had taken the waiting truck inland to Lukula, fifty-two miles along a hammered mud road that had been sliced out of the steaming jungle by ten thousand weary prisoners, taken out of the jails and told: Work, you bastards, or you don't eat.

There, their own plane had been waiting for them, secretly, on the now deserted airstrip that had once been used by the smugglers who brought their stolen diamonds up from the tightly guarded fields to the south, the Namib Desert of Southwest Africa, where thousands of stones lay right on the surface, ready to be picked up by any who would brave the machine guns and the dogs and the scouting helicopters of the vicious guards.

The plane was a Dassault Mirage III-R, extensively modified to hold, incredibly, five men who had been virtually slotted into their tight niches. The imposing array of Omera Type 31 cameras had been removed, and the new Aquarad had been fitted in their place. The twin 30mm. Defa 5–52 cannon had been taken out—the plane was completely unarmed and defenseless—and Paul Tobin was curled up like a fetus in the forward fuselage bay that had held the ammunition belts. The others—they were twisted into position, like corkscrews being eased into impenetrable spaces. Paul's left foot was tight by the navigator's ear.

But now they were on their way, flying at fourteen thousand feet over Bandundu, crossing over Kasai, easing

1

south to follow the invisible line of the Angolan border. The sky below them reflected the black of the ground, and the pilot said cheerfully: "Okay, this is where we start to get lost."

The navigator said: "Just watch that air speed, Moretti."

Moretti nodded. *"Butana Madonna,* how do they expect me to hit a black mountain in the middle of a black swamp that lies dead center in a black forest? On a black night . . ."

"We should have brought Betty de Haas along. She'd have found it for you."

Moretti laughed. *"Eh gia,* I wanted to bring her along. But for me, not for you."

The navigator sighed. "That's a tight little body she's got. A bit plump, but tight as a drum." His eyes were on the Aquarad co-ordinator, straining. "We're crossing over the Kaongeshi river now, more water on the left, must be the Lulua. Give me half a degree left, Moretti."

The pilot rubbed at the perspex helplessly and stared out. "Black, black, black."

"Half a degree, and hold her steady."

The plane bucked suddenly, savagely, and the navigator said: "Great, we're over the rift, dead on course. You're a good man, Moretti, for a bloody Italian."

He was young and bright-eyed, the navigator, a Maltese named George Drima who had been with Colonel Tobin's Private Army for less than a year. He peered at the radar screen and said: "Too loose, we're switching to Loran."

The Long Range Navigation System had been mounted aboard at the insistence of Betty de Haas in London, and Drima was grateful for her stubbornness. He took a rapid fix on Tangier to the northwest and Rhodes to the northeast, and pushed the computer button and said plaintively: "Put your brakes on, Moretti, let's stand still for a minute, make it a lot easier for me."

In a moment, he jotted the reading down on his chart and said: "That wasn't the Lulua—it was swamp water, not marked on the chart, back half a degree."

"Make your goddamn mind up," Moretti said.

2

The gentle, intermittent hum of the Aquarad raised its pitch slightly; they were following the line of the river now, and when it stopped abruptly, Drima said: "Give me a zig-zag, for Christ's sake. How am I supposed to navigate over uncharted swampland?"

Paul said: "Use your Astro-Intertial, that's what you're supposed to do."

Moretti grunted. He said: "He likes to make it hard for himself, a matter of pride. A bloody Maltese, what do you expect? The plane began a gentle swerving motion from side to side, and when the hum cut in, a deeper note now, Drima said happily: "The cataract; now hold her on a hundred and seventy-three point seven, think you can do that?"

Paul said: "The hell with it," and took hold of a stanchion and dragged himself out of his confined position, slewing round til his face was in Drima's lap. He eased a shoulder forward, reached under the Aquarad, twisted round until he was lying on his back, and said: "Drima, pour me a glass of the Irish, I'm too far from home. . . ."

He held out the Irish whisky bottle, the Colonel's trademark, and Drima grinned and held the tiny glass for him. It was a gardener's measuring glass, marked out in teaspoons for mixing insecticides, and Drima said, laughing to himself: "So much damned equipment jammed aboard, there wasn't even room for a decent glass."

Paul lay there and drank, lanky and slight and tough-looking, his yellow hair tousled, his freckled face shining in the blue light of the Aquarad. "How much further? I make it about twelve minutes."

Drima nodded. "Give or take a couple of hundred miles, yes."

"Oh?"

"Well, we'll make it. We've just passed the third cataract on the Kaongeshi."

"How's the Aquarad working out?"

"It's great."

It was still on the classified list, the Aquarad, and only Colonel Tobin's immense tenacity had overcome the difficulties that Washington had thrown at him when he had

3

asked for it. It would pick up water below the plane to a distance of forty thousand feet, estimate its depth, the speed of its movement if any, and its mineral content. "The hazel twig," Betty de Haas had called it, the water diviner, an immensely sophisticated piece of electronic gadgetry.

Drima said: "We should be heading straight for the eastern edge of the Kalene Range, coming up in twelve seconds . . ." He peered at the radarscope and said: Eight . . . six . . . four . . . yes, there it is . . . now. Great! Northern edge of the swamp should be forty miles ahead now." He looked at Paul. "We're going to have to do quite a bit of circling around once we hit that peak, and then . . . You realize just how accurate we've got to be?"

"I know."

"We've got to drop you on a plus-or-minus fifty-yard pinpoint. Fifty yards, for God's sake!"

"That's what all your nice expensive equipment is about."

"Fifty-one plus, and you're in quicksand. Fifty-one minus, and you're over the edge of the gorge."

"Just don't put us too close to the rim of the valley. There's a time element to worry about."

Moretti said: "Right in the middle, you have my word."

"Good."

"We might have to brush the tops off a few trees."

"Your problem, Moretti. . . ."

Drima said suddenly, startled: "A plane behind us—my God, where did he come from?" He recovered quickly and said: "Four thousand feet, dead astern, coming in fast, a fighter."

Paul said calmly: "Wait for identification, it could be Zambian or Congolese. What's our air speed?"

"Mach 1.21, nine hundred and twenty-five miles an hour. He's doing close on twelve hundred. Twin engine turbojet by the looks of it."

"That makes it, what, a Phantom?"

"Could be. Congolese Air Force, the RF–4B. I'm diving."

Paul said affably, squeezing himself back into position:

4

"Someone's supposed to say: Fasten your seat belts, please."

She was already in a steep dive, the Atar 8C3 turbojet roaring as Moretti thrust the throttle forward. By twisting his neck hard round he could read the altimeter, and when the needle reached a thousand feet and stayed there, the plane leveling out, he said mildly: "Three-thousand-foot mountains all around us, if I remember rightly."

Moretti nodded. He was about to speak when a ripping sound tore through the fuselage and the left-hand corner of the instrument panel shattered, and then the dark shape of the other plane swept across their front and up into the darkness, and Moretti said: "Just a farewell burst of machine-gun fire; he won't dare stay at this altitude. Anybody hurt?"

Paul quickly pushed the intercom plug home: "Talk, everybody."

There were two more of them back there somewhere, intertwined among the fuselage tighter than he was, Cass Fragonard, the Frenchman, and Aklilu Matende, the Ethiopian.

Fragonard said: "Okay here, Paul, I think Aklilu's hurt." And the deep-toned voice of the other man, very soft and gentle, came over the wire: "A scratch, Major, down one side of my leg, nothing to worry about."

"Sure about that?"

"I'm sure. In one ear and out the other, no problem."

Moretti said: "Just don't get blood all over the goddamn place, I like a clean plane."

Drima said: "And that's what it was, a Phantom, an RF-4B. I wonder why he didn't use his cannon, he could have knocked us to hell and gone out of the sky with one shell."

Paul grunted. "Chances are he was firing a warning burst across our bows. And missed."

"Goddamn, if I am going to get killed accidentally . . ."

"Are we still on course?"

Drima said: "Hell, no. We're miles off it now. I'll have to go back to Loran again when we get closer, is that all right with you?"

5

The Long Range Navigation System could be detected from the ground, but Paul shook his head and said: "No sweat, we're over the jungle. Use it all you want."

The Aquarad was humming again, and Drima checked the course and the chart and said: "That could be the Lunga, or one of the western tributaries of the Manyinga, take your pick. A lot of rivers down there now, and that Aquarad doesn't miss one of them, it's too damn sensitive." He looked at the scope and said: "Twin peaks coming up on the left, swamps to our right; my Christ, we're on course again, give or take a couple of miles."

Moretti said: "You could have stayed home in scenic Malta, Drima. We're dead on course. Why do you think they pay me so much money? Just because I can fly an airplane? Of course not, they pay for talent. Which raises a point. How come you're one of the group?"

The altimeter needle was creeping back to the three thousand mark, and he said: "When we find the spot, Paul, what height do you want to jump from?"

"Eight hundred feet?"

"Risky. The valley's only a hundred feet across at a couple of points."

"If you can fly through it . . . If you can find it . . ."

"Okay, eight hundred it is."

Paul spoke into the intercom again: "We're almost there. I go first, then Aklilu, then Cass, then Drima, and we keep it as tight as possible. You with me, Cass?"

Cass Fragonard said: *"Je suis lá, mon Commandant."*

"God alone knows what's down there. Trees, rocks, boulders . . . Are you going to be all right?"

Cass grinned and said: "You know me, Paul, I always carry a soldering iron." It was their standing joke. Cass had lost both his legs fighting the Riffs in Algeria, and now he walked on aluminum. *Cassoulet à pieds* they called him, the French cooking pot that stands on aluminum legs; Cass for short. He said: "You break a leg, Paul, just give me five minutes to hammer mine out straight, and I'll be there to help you."

They were wearing the oversize, thirty-three-foot parachutes that would drop them gently, like goose feathers, into whatever was waiting for them there. There would be no need for directional dropping; one pinpoint in the unknown darkness was as good as any other, provided it was within that hundred-yard circle.

The first of the green lights went on, a sign that the approximate area had been located, and Paul twisted around and looked at Drima's large-scale chart.

Drima's young, boyish fingers were tracing imaginary lines over it. He said: "This precise area has never been properly mapped, but Betty de Haas thinks that the northern slope of this hill ought to be about the best bet. If we can find it. You'll be right on the edge of the valley, she thinks there's a lot of manganese there and so there might be more open ground. At the same time . . ." He grimaced. "Nobody really knows. You just might find hundred-foot-high trees with ten-foot thorns sticking up from them. If you do, try not to find them the hard way, will you do that?" He jerked his thumb behind him. "Pinpoint's behind us now, Moretti's making sure he can take you down low enough."

Even in the darkness, acute and menacing, they could see the mountains flashing by them on both sides. See them? Or what is only a sense that told them they were there, dangerously close? They felt the plane turn and start climbing, and Moretti looked over his shoulder and said: "That's it, Paul. Ready when you are."

They checked their parachute harnesses, fingered the buttons that would eject them, like playing cards flipped out of a deck and sent spinning out into the unknown, and Paul said again: "Me, Aklilu, Cass, Drima, one two three four, about that speed. We've got to be close, tight, hand-in-hand."

The big Ethiopian said: "I take your parachute in my teeth, you will see."

Each of them was staring at his own particular light, burning green, and Moretti said: "Coming in now, eight hundred feet."

Drima said: "You'll be on your own, Moretti; you're going to get lost, as sure as hell. . . ." And then the first of the lights turned red and Paul touched the button and

7

felt the sudden rush of cold air as the slip-stream hit him, and for one crazy moment he thought: "My God, did I hitch up the static line?"

He was rolling over, and he flung out his arms and legs to stop the movement, and then he was floating in space and the plane was climbing high above him on its way back to Lukula, to Moanda, and on to its home in the south of England.

He felt, with a shock, a steel-tough grip on his shoulder, and turned his head to see Aklilu grinning at him and saying delightedly: "Close enough, Paul?"

He threw back his head and laughed suddenly in the silence, and saw that Cass was on his left, Drima a little further away, hauling in a rope to bring him closer. And then, the top of a tall tree rushed up at him, the parachute snagged and ripped, and he hung there swinging gently from side to side. He looked down and saw that Aklilu had landed well, and he began to swing harder, groping for the trunk and finding it. There was no hand hold, so he unwound the nylon rope to the ground, slapped the harness buckle with the flat of his hand, and slid down the rope to the soft mud at the base of the tree.

Drima was already at work with the first-aid kit on Aklilu's leg. The bullets had carved twin rivulets of blood down the outside of the calf, and Drima was plucking out a tiny sliver of bone, but the Ethiopian was grinning, looking up at the parachute in the tree, and saying: "You want me to get it for you, Paul?"

Aklilu and Cass had already unslung their rifles.

Paul tapped the broad, smooth trunk, soft as the flesh of an apple. He said: "Boabab, I can make it."

He pulled out his hunting knife and cut a dozen heavy twigs, and drove them into the soft trunk with the flat face of a heavy stone, then climbed up into the upper branches, using the twigs as a ladder. It took him ten minutes to free the torn chute, and he rolled it up and tossed it down to Cass, then clambered down again, pulling out the rungs of his ladder as he descended and tossing them into the hole that Cass was digging for the parachutes. No one was likely to pass this deserted way, but if someone did, the sharp-cut ends of the twigs would betray an alien presence.

He looked at his watch: four thirty-nine. Was that the beginnings of the dawn over there? A faint grey streak, or only his imagination? Aklilu had picked up a handful of mud and was squelching it through his powerful fingers, and Paul looked at him and said: "Footprints?"

Alkilu shook his head. "Too soft. In a few moments, they will have gone. Up there it will be different." He pointed. "Up there, where the red flowers are."

Paul stared. "Red flowers?"

There was nothing but the black of the mountain, and Aklilu grinned and said: "You do not have African eyes. Red flowers, hibiscus, I think. Dry sand to sleep on. And perhaps I can even catch us something to eat for breakfast." It was a point of honor with him never to eat the concentrated food they always carried with them, not in the bush, at least. He said, grinning: "In your skyscraper jungles, I will eat your malted milk tablets and your damn space foods, but here . . . here, we will have steak for breakfast."

Paul said: "So lead on, Hawk-eye."

They fell in behind him, and slowly climbed up the steep wall of the valley. When they reached hard ground Aklilu cut a branch with his bush knife and gave it to Drima, the last man, to drag behind him to wipe out their footprints.

And when the grey streak in the east had become a reality and was turning to golden red, three of them were lying asleep under the cover of the pungent wild basil bushes.

Only Paul was awake, crouched in the branches of an umbrella thorn, his rifle beside him, the powerful Trinovid binoculars to his eyes as he waited, and watched, and listened to the bush sounds all around him.

Once there was the cough of a leopard, the snarl of an angry baboon, and the raucous shriek of a monkey. He could hear the splashing of hippopotamus down there in the swamp they had left behind them.

9

Now all they had to do was pick out a landing ground for the others.

And then, a little later, he caught the glint of reflected sun over there in the west, a single flash that shone brightly and was gone. A mirror? A bright flash of metal? A heliograph?

He began to think about it.

CHAPTER TWO

LONDON
CO-ORDINATES: 00.00E
51.50N

The sun, for a change, was shining brightly, casting a pale yellow glow over the remnants of the mist that still hung, tenaciously, over the chestnut trees that shaded the verandah.

Colonel Matthew Tobin pushed aside the dish of kidneys and bacon that his servant Charles had prepared for him, drained his third cup of strong black coffee, and went back into his bedroom to dress.

When he was ready, he pressed the button on the intercom and said: "Charles? It's eight o'clock exactly, Mr. Jendoro should be here." He waited a moment, and then: "He is? Good, I'll be right down. I think perhaps you'd better join us, and I want Betty de Haas standing by as well. What sort of man is Jendoro?"

The voice over the speaker box was low, controlled, very sure: "Well, my first impression, sir . . ."

"That's what I want, a first impression."

"I'd say a good man. Quite in keeping with the file we have on him. Not as strong, perhaps, on the surface, but a certain stubbornness if you look hard enough. Not a man to fool around with, I'd say."

"A chip on his shoulder? That's what I really want to know."

Charles said: "No sir, I don't think so. On the contrary, I got the impression of—a kind of tolerance that can't be pushed too far."

"I'll be down in a few minutes; you might bring coffee. Are the maps in position?"

"Of course."

"Good." He switched off and stared at his face in the

11

mirror for a while, stroking the underside of his chin and feeling for any incipient slack; there was none. A sun-burned, light weight, wiry sort of man with the ice-blue eyes that his son Paul had inherited from him, a restless air reflected in them, the kind of restlessness that wouldn't let him sit down for more than a few minutes at a time.

He turned and strode briskly out of the room and down the blue-carpeted stairway to the paneled lounge that was the center of his whole world.

He put on his most affable smile, held out his hand, and said: "Mr. Jendoro, I'm sorry if I kept you waiting."

His guest was standing by the window, looking out across the lawn and the rose bed, and he turned and came to meet the Colonel, moving easily, lightly, a controlled spring in his step. The Colonel was mentally checking over the file: "Five feet eight, thickset, a hundred and eighty pounds, born November seventh, 1928, educated University of Leopoldville, the Sorbonne, and Cambridge. . . ."

Jendoro's grip was hard, yet delicate, the grip of a man who knows his strength and is careful with it, and he said, smiling: "I may be wasting my time, Colonel Tobin, which is not important. More to the point, I may be wasting yours."

"Kind of you to phrase it like that. I've ordered coffee, I'm sure you'd like some."

"Thank you, I would indeed." There was a slight hesitation, and then: "I take it you must know precisely who I am, and what I represent, or you wouldn't have agreed to see me?"

The Colonel said smoothly: "I know you to be the Prime Minister of Kamapa, which I know to be one of the emerging—is that the current word?—African states. What you represent—that's altogether another question, isn't it? Suppose you tell me, first, who gave you my name?"

Jendoro was smiling gently. He said: "A confidence, I'm afraid, that I cannot break. Will it suffice if I say he's at the Ministry of Defense in Whitehall?"

"Ah yes. At the Ministry they like to pretend I don't exist. They just—send people to me. You're concerned, no

12

doubt about the incipient invasion of your country by a rebel army from Zambia?"

Jendoro was startled. "You know about that?"

The Colonel nodded. "I know that an offensive fellow named Major Dogger, a mercenary of dubious origins . . . ." He broke off smiling. "Oh yes, I'm a mercenary too, but of an entirely different kind, as you must know. I have been told that Dogger has gathered a disreputable army of swashbucklers, and is eyeing Kamapa's diamond fields with a greedy eye. I have been told that the Zambian army tried to stop him on their own territory, and failed. I know that your own army is not strong enough to contain him. Ergo, I assume that's what you came to see me about."

Jendoro said: "And you know, too, about General Guevara Lincoln?"

The Colonel's eyebrows shot up. "*Guevara* Lincoln? No. But with a name like that, maybe I *should* know about him. Who is he?"

The Prime Minister hesitated. He said at last: "Would it appear discourteous if I asked about your—legality, first? When the British Defense Ministry mentioned your army, I made a few inquiries of my own, and—it's a rather clandestine operation you run, isn't it?"

"If you mean you found no answers, I'm very glad to hear it. And yes, I'm legal. I operate a private army, the smallest, the best, the toughest army in the world, and I operate it with the tacit blessings of most of the Western powers, even if they prefer to pretend I don't exist. The days of gunboat diplomacy are gone, Prime Minister, and no country, today, can afford to show the flag, to send out the Marines to intervene in another country's affairs. In the last fifty years, expeditionary forces have been despatched, as you must know, to almost every country in the world. Not any more, it's too dangerous. Today they call me in and pretend they know nothing about what I do." He smiled quickly. "Yes, I'm legal. Though I don't really believe it would worry you too much if I weren't."

"No, perhaps not. We face a desperate situation . . ."

Behind him, Jendoro heard the door open, and he turned instinctively to see a tall, svelte, blonde-haired and

13

very beautiful woman standing there, a silver tray of coffee in her hands. She wore a tight-fitting black sheath dress that might almost, but not quite, have been a servant's uniform, very short indeed, and she had the longest legs he had ever seen.

Colonel Tobin said offhandedly: "I think you met my man Charles, Prime Minister." As she came forward, he said: "My private secretary, my personal assistant, my housekeeper, butler, anything else you can think of, and my *confidante*. Prime Minister Obote Jendoro, Pamela Charles."

She almost swayed towards him when she had put down the tray, and she took his hand and smiled. He bowed to cover his confusion, and said: "Yes, of course, we half met, if that's the phrase. A great pleasure, Miss Charles."

He watched the articulation of her hips as she moved to pour the coffee, and the Colonel said: "Tell me about *Guevara* Lincoln. How in hell did he get a name like that? And just who is he?"

Charles had gone to the map case and was pulling down the large-scale map of Central Africa; Jendoro looked at it and said: "My God, I've never seen a map of my country as detailed as that." He lifted the corner and looked at the others, and said, drawing in his breath: "They are beautiful. I wish you'd tell me where you get them."

Colonel Tobin shrugged. "Our own cartographers. We have the American satellite maps to draw on, the old British maps, the old French maps, the reports of the National Geographic Society . . . We just make sure that we keep them up to date. Who, and what, is Guevara Lincoln?"

Jendoro sighed. "I don't really know who he is. A rumor, a cypher, and a distinctive threat. Our own Intelligence is somewhat limited, but it seems that quite a massive army is moving into Kamapa from the west, as well as the rebel army under Major Dogger from the south. . . ."

The Colonel said sharply: "The west? That means Angola. The Angolan Government? Surely not. They have enough worries of their own as it is."

"No, not the Angolans. They give us a headache too, from time to time, but this is something quite different.

14

We believe them to be a force made up of several different rebel groups, an amalgamation of dissident tribes who have been brought together under one man, a leader who seems to have been able to persuade them to forget their mutual animosities and unite under his generalship. These little violent bands are usually no more than a hundred or two strong, but now . . . The latest reports, probably exaggerated, speak of eight thousand men."

"And Dogger, in the south, has about ten thousand. That's interesting."

Jendoro looked at him curiously. He said: "I'm surprised you know about Major Dogger, Colonel."

Colonel Tobin's face was hard. "We know *all* about him. Karl Sebastian Dogger, ex-Foreign Legion, a sergeant, and a very bad one, personally responsible for a great number of atrocities in Algeria. He was fighting in Biafra, tried to change sides when they started losing the war, and the Nigerians refused his help. Before that he was with Tschombe in the Congo, and was thrown out of there because of some particularly brutal murders. He fought with the Arabs against the Central Government of Chad, and with the Sudanese against the Egyptians, trying to change sides once more when the Egyptians started winning. He was finally captured in Uganda, escaped, and came to me for a job."

The memory was still ripe in his mind. He said grimly: "My son, Paul, was in London at the time, and they got into a fist fight, right here in this room. He's a violent and impulsive man, Dogger, and I'm happy to say that Paul beat the hell out of him and threw him out into the street. A mercenary of the worst kind."

He saw the look on Jendoro's face and said piously: "Oh yes, quite definitely there are two quite disparate *kinds* of mercenary soldiers, and I belong to the *best* kind, so forgive me if I use the word with contempt on one occasion and approbation on another. The world has not yet reached that happy state in which it can dispense with the services of armed men, and until it does, some of us are on the side of right, and some are on the side of profit, Now, Guevara Lincoln. Is it your presumption—not that I care

15

for presumptions except as a starting point—that he'll link up with Dogger's men? That would make a powerful army, a very dangerous threat."

Jendoro shook his head. "No, Colonel, I think not. It seems to us that Dogger is determined to wipe General Lincoln's army off the face of Africa. And that General Lincoln has the same idea about Dogger."

The Colonel said slowly: "I see. And Kamapa is to be the battleground. You really do need me, don't you?"

Jendoro nodded eagerly. "You see, Colonel Tobin? If these two forces meet together in the jungles of my country, the only possible victim is going to be my people. It's not a question of whether or not they take sides, brother against brother perhaps, or most certainly tribe against tribe. It's simply the devastation that is going to reduce us to . . . to another Biafra. And I won't allow it. One way or another, I'm going to stop it."

The Colonel said again: "I see."

For a while he fell silent, standing at the window with its dark blue velvet drapes, and listening to the faint rumble of the morning traffic. He said at last: "Guevara Lincoln, *General* Lincoln, he's the key, isn't he? Get on the blower, Charles, we might have something about him tucked away somewhere."

He heard her soft, low voice talking into the intercom: "Guevara Lincoln, General, Africa, that's all we have. But it should be enough. If you have anything at all, send it down right away. And start the ball rolling for more details, it's urgent."

He liked the way she took the responsibility upon herself; whether or not he took the assignment, she knew that one day, sooner or later, *any* man posing an individual threat might become an enemy of the Private Army.

He studied the map for a while, tracing lines across it with the thin mahogany baton, and said at last: "Your population—what is it, about a million and a half?"

Jendoro nodded. "A trifle more, perhaps. We have no census."

The Colonel was thumbing through the glossary. "In an area of three hundred and two thousand square miles,

16

that's pretty thinly spread. Ethnic groups: Bantu, Pigmy, Hamitic, Semitic, Hamito-Semitic, and a Nilotic minority—where did they come from, I wonder? Religions: mostly animist, fifteen percent Christian, three percent Moslem. Economy: agricultural, cotton, coffee, forest products. Exports limited to small amounts of gold and tungsten, and diamonds. Languages: Swahili, French, English and thirty-nine local dialects. And all your people are spread out in limited areas, along the main rivers. Forests, swamp, desert, and mountains—you've got everything, haven't you?"

There was a knock on the door, and he saw Charles push the button that would unlock it and light up the green lamp in the hall. A young girl entered, a slim young teen-ager with long dark hair and bright, alert eyes. She went quickly to Charles and handed her a file, then smiled quickly at the Colonel and went out again. Charles leafed through the pages, speed-reading them, then looked up and said: "Guevara Lincoln, real name unknown, ex-member of the Black Panthers in New York . . ."

The Colonel said, surprised: "An American?"

She nodded. "So it seems. Thrown out of the Panthers for murdering one of their more important leaders, took refuge in Algeria, thrown out of there for inciting a riot against the police, disappeared for two years, turned up in Cameroon, where he was to raise an army to invade Gabon. Wanted by the New York police on murder charges, in California for murder, Libya for murder, and Angola, also for murder. He sounds like a rather violent man."

She held out the file to the Colonel, but he shook his head and said: "No, show it to me when it's complete."

He was frowning at the map again. "Absolute secrecy, that's the only way I'd consider it, or the odds would not be acceptable. Your back country's unexplored; we'd have to send out an advance party at night, a handful of men. There wouldn't be much room for passengers in the Mirage, would there, but we need its range . . ." He was thinking aloud, and Jendoro waited. The Colonel said to Charles: "Get Betty for me, will you?"

17

He turned to Jendoro and smiled. "Betty de Haas, without a doubt the world's best cartographer. She is responsible for the maps you like so much; I'll have her send over a set for you."

Jendoro inclined his head. "You are very kind, Colonel."

He heard Charles speak into the intercom, and in a moment Betty de Haas was there, a dark-haired, plump, attractive young woman in her early thirties, bouncing braless and walking with quick, short steps on very high heels, the inevitable roll of maps under her plump little arm.

The Colonel made the introductions and said briefly: "Kamapa. Natural obstacles for an invading army. From the south."

She pulled down the third of the maps in the case, the larger scale, and taking the baton, pointed and said: "The Kalene Range, running east to west for a hundred and thirty miles, cut through with very deep gorges, no tracks of any sort going right through it unless they use the defiles here, here and here. A very small force on the peaks here could hold off almost any number of troops indefinitely, unless they were attacked from the air. Not an insuperable obstacle, but a very tough one."

"And barriers from the west?"

She said promptly: "The swamps, they're very treacherous. Depending on where the invading force originated, they'd have to go round them to the north, over the Lupweiji River, which is one long line of cataracts, or south across the Kalene foothills, which might be easier."

The Colonel said, squinting at the map: "The top of the Kalene Range, that's about seven thousand feet on the average; if an army were in position there . . . where would you try to hit them, from the north or from the south? The north, by the looks of it."

She nodded, a quick, urgent sort of gesture. "Yes, of course. You'd never make it from the south, it's too rugged. Unless you air-lifted your troops."

"Water supplies, no problem?"

"No, none. Plenty of water everywhere. Not very good, but it can be treated if necessary."

"But up on the Kalene Range an army could have no lines of communication of any sort. That presupposes a certain degree of self-sufficiency. Is there plenty of game?"

"Oh yes, they can live off the land easily enough."

"All right." He took the baton from her and tapped it against the map. "I want a territorial run-down on these three areas: The Angolan, Congolese, and Zambian borders. I want to know every river, every forest, every valley, every hill, every village, every track leading to or from anything or nothing. And I want it soon. I also want to know where I can parachute a couple of men, without any fear of discovery, about equidistant in terms of *time* from the western and southern borders. As soon as possible, please."

She nodded, and hurried briskly out, and Jendoro said somberly: "I take it, Colonel Tobin, that you will come to my aid?"

"I will, Prime Minister."

He hesitated. "We have not discussed finances, have we? We are not a rich country, but . . ."

The Colonel shrugged. "Send one of your secretaries over in a day or two when my computers have had a chance to do some costing. You have a small standing army of your own, I won't need them. I will require that no word of my activities, no word at all, be given to any of your associates, even at the ministerial level. Is that acceptable?"

"Yes, Colonel, it is."

"You have an Air Force, I believe?"

Jendoro grimaced. "If you can call it that. Four Lysanders and a Handley-Page."

"The Congolese and the Angolans are well armed with American aircraft. If I decide to use planes I'll use my own, but I may want to borrow your colors."

"Agreed, of course."

"If any activity is required on your part, Prime Minister, I will let you know. Apart from that, you must take no action of any kind. I will take care of your problem in my own way. With no prodding, no brakes, and no interfer-

19

ence. If I sound harsh, forgive me, but the lives of many people are at stake."

Jendoro nodded. "I understand, Colonel Tobin. And I offer you the thanks of my country."

"Thank me when it's over, Prime Minister."

"I will, sir."

Jendoro hesitated, studying Colonel Tobin's features, seeing how ice-cold the pale blue eyes were. He said: "My ministers wanted me to approach the UN for assistance. I was in Washington before I came here. Not only did they turn me down, but—somehow—I came away with the impression that if the Organization of African States had taken up my case we might have had a third rampaging army in our land, holding the other two at bay. I must say that the prospect shocked me. I had visions of . . ." he gestured vaguely. " . . . of half my country defoliated, the crops on which our peasants live destroyed to save those peasants from the likes of Major Dogger and General Lincoln. I'm glad I came to you instead."

"My army," Colonel Tobin said, "doesn't go on the rampage. We use a rapier, not a broadsword. We use our wits as well as our arms, and we use them well. I promise you that your people will not suffer." He smiled quickly and held out his hand. "That's what makes me a *good* mercenary, Prime Minister."

When Jendoro had gone, he looked at Charles and said: "Paul's coming in this evening, isn't he?"

"Yes sir. He wanted to dine with you at the Ecu de France. I've reserved a table."

"Ah, good." He thumped his taut stomach hard, and said: "Dammit. I'm getting flabby. Give me a rubdown, Charles, will you?"

"All right."

She pulled down the leather-padded cot from its niche in the carved walnut paneling, spread the white sheet out over it, and said: "I'll get the things."

She went out softly, and he stripped down to bare skin and lay on the cot on his back and worried about Kamapa and two violent antagonists who would soon be his own, about two angry, ambitious men who soon would be clashing over an impoverished, frightened country that was trying so hard to pull itself out of the past by its own bootstraps, a country that soon—unless he acted quickly—would be tasting the terror and the tragedy of brutal, African-style warfare.

Charles came back in a little while, dressed in a short black kimono of heavy silk. She put down the alcohol and the oil and the vibrator on the beautiful teak table, and began kneading his stomach muscles with strong, firm hands, well-trained and capable.

He touched her long smooth calf with the tips of his fingers, and ran them up under the short kimono and over her naked hip. A useless gesture, he was thinking; he'd slept with Betty de Haas that night, and Betty was an exigent and exhausting woman.

The point of her hip was almost sharp, no flesh on it at all, just a smooth covering of taut, exciting alabaster. He said: "You're too damn sensuous for your own good, Charles. You know that, don't you?"

Her hands did not stop working. "Yes sir."

"If you weren't so damned efficient I'd fire you."

"Yes sir."

"And when we're through, get out the file on Major Dogger; I want to take a long hard look at it."

"Yes sir."

He closed his eyes, enjoying the touch of her hands, and let the euphoria blot out the rest of the world.

CHAPTER THREE

KOTOLOKI
CO-ORDINATES: 22.38E
           12.07S

Even at this early hour the heat of the sun was sucking at their life's blood, but drawing out, instead, all the moisture in their bodies. The air was humid, oppressive, no breath of wind anywhere.

The ground was rugged, harshly broken by deep ravines and jagged outcrops of blue stone in which great chunks of shining zircon were embedded, red, yellow, orange, blue; some of it was green as jade, some of it translucent as diamonds.

The yellow sand was dotted with clumps of rubber vine and tall acacia stands. And towering hills, built by millions upon millions of warrior ants, threw their pinnacles for thirty or forty feet into the bright, hot sky, as blue as cobalt. A few white clouds were scattered there, motionless puffs of cotton.

Paul Tobin stared at a thick knee-joint of brilliant zircon, bipyramid, prismatic, tetragonal, jutting out of a rock like a diamond the size of his shoulder. Was the bright light he had seen out there more of this zircon? He thought not; to flash like that it would have to have moved.

He turned to Drima, who was using his Trinovid binoculars, covering the horizons around him. "All right, Drima, you're the expert. Where are we?"

The young Maltese navigator felt ill at ease. He was sure that this was a test for him, part of the growing up process of the Private Army. He was conscious that Paul was watching him closely.

He pointed. "The edge of the swamp lies eight and a half miles over the rim of the valley, there. It stretches for a hundred and forty miles east to west, right across our fron, eighty miles wide at its widest point, thirteen at its narrowest. The forest behind us covers seventy-two miles east to west, a hundred and twelve north to south. On our left, the cataracts of the Lupweiji River . . ."

"How far?"

"Fourteen miles, a little more maybe."

"And Mount Ngaru?"

Drima grinned. "Forty-six degrees exactly from here, a distance of thirty-one miles to the peak."

"Then the sun's half a degree off this morning."

"No sir. We're twelve degrees south of the Equator."

"All right, good enough. Villages?"

"The nearest is Kotoloki, between here and the Lup-weiji, eight miles."

"Population?"

"Believed abandoned after the floods last year, possibly reoccupied, probably about thirty families. Nobody else within a hundred miles or so, except any tribesmen wandering along the banks of the river, and the trading post."

"Good." He turned to Aklilu, standing there patiently, his eyes, too, constantly searching the horizons around him. "Leg all right?"

The Ethiopian nodded. "Yes sir."

"You take the left flank, about three miles out. Cass takes the right. Drima and I in the center and we'll keep a little ahead of you. Keep your receivers open at all times. I want to rendezvous on the slopes of the mountain by dark, and that gives us about eleven and a half hours. You all know what to look for—so let's start looking. Silently."

No one around, Drima had said, and he was probably right. But it was impossible to be sure; a runner from one village to another, a scout for Dogger's army—or Guevara Lincoln's—on the tireless jog from one outpost to the next . . . it behooved them to keep hidden.

Cass was already moving towards the forest, so dense that it was a black-green morass of humid, impenetrable, threatening danger. Cass would move slower than the others, cutting his way through.

In spite of the leg wound, Aklilu was running lightly

over to the left, up the slope towards the lip beyond which the swamp lay. He moved like an animal, walking in the shade where the bushes were, then running fast across the open patches of sunlight, the shadows speckling his body; the camouflage jeans were brown and green, with a splash here and there of deep maroon, like wine-stains—or bloodstains, Paul was thinking.

He turned to look at Drima. "We have the easy way."

"No sir. Quicksand ahead of us, a lot of it."

"We'll manage."

A lone baboon was on the rocks ahead of them, peering at them intently, and Paul said: "Their sentry; there'll be a whole herd of them in there somewhere." The baboon was grey with age, and his lips were drawn back to show the huge yellow teeth, a warning to keep away. They moved steadily towards him, slipping from boulder to boulder, looking for the hard ground, checking that they left no spoor.

Cass and Aklilu had disappeared altogether, and Paul spoke into the tiny mike at his throat, its capillary wire leading to the micro-miniaturized set in the breast pocket of his camouflage suit.

"Come in, Cass, Aklilu."

"I'm over the rim," Aklilu said, "the swamp down below doesn't look very inviting."

Paul adjusted the ear plug, easing it round. "I'd like to know more about it, see how deep it is. Cass?"

The Frenchman said: "*Mon Dieu*, nobody can move in this, nobody. I'm keeping to the edge, you can't get more than a few feet in."

"Then come out, move on, try further up. I want a pattern, that's all. Cut your way deep in round about midday, let me know what it looks like."

They moved on. The land about them was red-brown, hard-packed sandstone intermixed with volcanic lava, cut with deep fissures that gave them shelter from the broiling sun. Here and there a thorn tree towered out of the hot earth, and they found a pool of deep, cold water and soaked themselves in it, and moved on again, heading for the slopes of the mountain.

The trees closed about them, and they used their machetes carefully, slicing through only enough of the tightly tangled vines to give them passage.

At eleven o'clock, Aklilu's voice came over the walkie-talkie, so close and clear that it startled him: "Are you there, Paul? The swamp's mostly impenetrable; I tried eight different places and found only one where I could stand more or less safely, up to my waist, say a little over three feet. Further in, it looks softer, I'd say no one could cross it. But I found a canoe, abandoned, a hundred years old at least, rotting to pieces. A solid piece of teak, ten feet long. There's flat sandstone ahead of me now, about three miles of it, tall trees at both ends. Might be a good place."

"All right, mark it."

"It's marked."

"Cass?"

Cass said: *"Je suis là, comme toujours,* on-the-spot Cass, they call me."

"Anything?"

"Monkeys. A million monkeys. I found a trail, cut a few months ago, by the looks of it—it's hard to tell. Anyway, all grown over again, very hard to see except in patches. Just a single trail, one man or a single file. And there's a fire burning ahead of me somewhere, I can smell it."

"I see the smoke," Paul said. "A small forest fire. I like it."

Cass was startled. "You like it? *Fragonard roti,* is that what you want?"

"The wood's too wet to burn much, don't worry about it. But fires are good, we'll have to burn the glider. Keep moving."

"Marchons, marchons, q'un sang impur . . ."

They moved on. Bamboo forest now, some of it more than a hundred feet high, and they eased their way through it, rustling the stalks. Drima said, panting hard: "Two miles of this, according to Betty."

Paul had stopped to examine the young shoots that emerged from the damp soil like phalli, a million of them sprouting. He cut one with his bush knife and tossed it to

26

Drima and said: "Does that look to you like the sensors?"

Drima turned it over and over. He nodded. "They made a pretty good job of them, Major."

The sensors were the directional-finders that would be spiked into the ground at intervals wherever tracks were found; some of them would merely pick up the sound of moving men and relay it, while others, more sophisticated—and much more expensive—would relay voices for monitoring on the master at the base. Their range was thirty miles.

Drima said: "How many will we be using, Paul?"

Paul shrugged. "As many as we need. Four, five hundred perhaps. Bramble will bring them in when he comes."

They found their way out of the bamboo and looked out at the soft white sea ahead of them—shimmering pale-grey sand that stretched to the left and to the right of them for as far as they could see. Paul took the binoculars and studied it; in parts, the sand grains were moving, bubbling gently over each other.

He said to Drima: "There's your quicksand."

Drima nodded. "More than a mile across; we'll have to find a way round it."

"No. We cross it, or try to. If we can then they can too, and that's something I want to know about. We need four good branches, Y-shaped if possible, seven or eight feet long." He pointed. "Over there."

Drima, trying not to show his alarm, went over and hacked at the acacia trees, and Paul shaped the cut branches the way he wanted them, smooth to the bark, no sharp twigs to impede their sliding. He tossed one of them onto the sand, and it lay there, and he put the other down beside it and lay between them on his belly, his arms across the supports, gently sliding them along as he wormed his way across. His long legs were sinking, being sucked down, and he squirmed them to one side, examining the ground ahead of him minutely, watching for the patches where it seemed to boil.

When he had gone a hundred feet, he twisted round gently and looked back at Drima, standing there and watching him anxiously. "Your rope now, cast it over to me."

The nylon rope came snaking over, and he wound an end of it round his wrist and said: "Now, follow my tracks while they last, go exactly where I go. Keep as much of your body as possible in contact with the sand, slide your supports along too. If one of them starts to sink, abandon it and slide away from it. Keep the rope taut at all times."

Slowly, painfully, they slid their way across. Once Drima felt his shoulders going down dangerously fast, and he yelled his alarm; Paul tugged on the rope and eased him out, and together they moved onwards.

The bubbling patches were more frequent now, gigantic sand clocks with the grains pouring down to infinity. How long had it been going on? Centuries? Aeons?

Two hours later they came to the other edge, and climbed gratefully to their feet. They tossed their supports back into the sea where the bubbling was greatest, and watched as they were sucked down quickly, out of sight, and Paul nodded and said: "Well, they *can* cross if they have to. But no one in his right mind's going to try it."

Drima was shaking. He shuddered. "I hope I never have to do that again."

Now it was easy going, a narrow open space ahead of them, too shallow to be called a valley. It was gently rolling, hemmed in on three sides by steep cliffs and dissected by a wide, shallow river that twisted in and out among the granite boulders. At one end, a thick stand of umbrella thorns, seventy, eighty feet high, formed a wide crescent from side to side, a dense canopy suspended high in the air by the gnarled and twisted trunks.

They followed the line of the river till it swung round under the trees, a long and wide tunnel of deep shade, and Paul said: "Perfect. Now let's get to the top of the hill."

He waited while Drima took the precise co-ordinates, grinning at him and saying: "We've made twenty-two miles in eight hours and ten minutes; that's not bad over that kind of terrain." He was sweating profusely, the stain darkening his camouflage suit. He said at last: "Twenty-two forty-one east, twelve-nine south; they can come in on a finder—nearly four hundred yards of runway, it's great. Nine miles to the peak, it's going to be a hard climb."

The land rose sharply now, bright red and splashed with dense green vegetation, a great red gash across the front where a landslide had brought down a million tons of sand and rock from the top, packed with up-ended trees and giant ferns.

Paul pointed: "There, the third level, that's the point we need, not much more than a hundred feet to the peak from there. All right, get your finder placed."

Drima scouted the ground, walking back from under the shade of the trees to the end of the little valley where the quicksand began, then walked back slowly, his eyes on the ground, and placed the box with the finder in it carefully under a small rock. He unscrewed the activator, closed up the box again, and piled deep sand over it. He tossed a fallen branch on top and said: "Ready for activation, sir."

"So let's move on."

Paul spoke quietly into his mike: "Cass? Aklilu? The west side of the peak, a hundred feet below it, a heavy stand of bananas. Can either of you see it?"

Cass answered him first: "A small boy lost in the forest, *mon Commandant,* I see nothing, nothing but a tangle of lianas trying to strangle me. But I'll find it."

"Aklilu?"

"I see it."

"I'll be waiting for you there. We've found a landing strip. Come on in when you're ready."

Wearily they clambered up the steep mountainside, pulling themselves up with the exposed roots of trees, kicking back loose sand to obliterate their footprints.

They reached the first level, more bamboo here, and climbed over a high smooth peak of blue granite, using the ropes and the pitons. They cut their way up steep banks, climbed a small cataract of ice-cold, refreshing water, slung a rope over a ravine and traversed it, passed across the second level with ease, and as the last half of the red sun went down and the shadow crept up from the valley below and enveloped them, they cut their way into the dense banana forest and sank, exhausted, to the ground. They were panting hard, both of them, drenched in sweat from their exertions.

Drima said: "I hear water."

Paul nodded. "Over there. Let's go find it."

The twilight was only a few moments long, and when they found the stream, four feet deep and splashing gently over bright-washed pebbles, the night had come. They stripped off their clothes and wallowed in the water and then Aklilu was there, grinning at them in the darkness and getting out of his camouflage suit, his black, muscular body gleaming in the bright light of the moon.

Paul clambered out and stood on the bank, naked, letting the breeze play about him, and reached for his walkie-talkie.

He said: "Cass? Where the hell are you?"

The voice was loud and clear: *"Perdu, comme toujours. . . . I* must be five hundred meters below you, *mon Commandant."*

"All right, switch to directional finder and come on in. You need help?"

"No sir, *j'arrive.* Give me ten or fifteen minutes."

"Switching to DF. Out."

He turned the lever on the box to the DF mark, placed it on a rock, lay back on the soft green moss and waited. And when Cass arrived and plunged fully clothed into the stream, Paul took the silver flask from the pocket of his suit, unscrewed the top, and handed it round.

He said: "Four hours to go till Bramble comes in, and everything's ready, the way it should be. Let's all have some of the Colonel's Irish whisky."

Aklilu said: "Reports?"

"We'll wait till Bram gets here. He'll want to know it all too."

Cass said: "Me, I stay in my bath until that happy moment."

Two hours to get back to the landing ground, lighter now with the equipment stashed away up here; one hour to make sure there was time to spare. One hour, then, to rest and relax and take it easy. They were lucky.

Paul looked at his watch and closed his eyes. He said: "In sixty minutes exactly, we move on down again."

There was nothing to do now but wait.

CHAPTER FOUR

MOUNT NGARU
CO-ORDINATES: 22.40E
               12.05S

Major Bramble had never felt so uncomfortable. He hated parachuting more than anything else in the world.

Betty de Haas had said to him in London: "Paul will have found a suitable landing place, there'll be no problem. Their drop's a hard one, but the support party . . ." She smiled at him, aware of his discomfort; had it only been six hours ago? "There'll be a finder for you to go in on. Paul's not going to let you drop in the swamp."

"Oh, I've no worries on that score," he told her. He couldn't keep his eyes off her breasts, the nipples hard under the tight cashmere sweater; the urge to reach out and touch them was almost insupportable. He said, lying brazenly: "As a matter of fact, I rather like parachuting. It's exhilarating."

"Uh-huh." She was gathering up her maps, a tidy little gesture, with neat, meticulous movements, putting them just so. He thought the burnt-orange color she was wearing today was good for her. She said primly: "You can only make one run, you know, because we don't want to advertise our presence any more than we have to. It's bad enough that Paul had to fly around for so long, but that was unavoidable; the ground's quite unknown out there. Did you know that they got machine-gunned? A Congolese Air Force plane took a crack at them."

"Yes, I heard."

"Equipment?"

"All ready for loading."

"Checked over, I take it?"

"Twice."

33

They'd been sitting together at the map table in Betty's office on the third floor of the Colonel's lovely old house, and Pamela Charles was there, unobtrusive but *there,* checking over the staff records. The thick file she was working on was lettered in the same script as that used on the door's bronze plaque: *BETTY de HAAS: CARTOGRAPHY.* He looked at her long, long legs, sheer and smooth as alabaster, then back at Betty's plump little body, and thought to himself: How happy could I be with either . . .

He had said, more loudly than necessary: "Not much time before we take off . . ." and Pamela Charles, just as unobtrusively, had left the room. When the door had softly closed, he had whispered: "We have forty minutes, can we go to your room?"

She'd been very cool indeed, but blushing nicely. "This is my room, Major Bramble."

"I know, but . . ." He swallowed hard. "Your bedroom."

"At five o'clock in the afternoon? Most certainly not."

But she leaned over and kissed him lightly on the cheek, and he held her breast for a moment, and then he stood up abruptly and said: "Well, got to get on that damned plane, I suppose. Who's the pilot?"

"Moretti again."

"Ah, splendid. He's a good man."

He hoisted his personal pack onto the broad bulk of his shoulder, and went down the stairs and onto the street where the car was waiting. It was Colonel Tobin's personal Rolls, and he was touched.

Now the damned plane was bucking savagely, even at this height, and he went forward into the cockpit and said to Moretti: "For God's sake, are we all right?"

He liked to keep an eye on the two Rolls-Royce Avon 109 turbojets to make sure they weren't both falling off.

Moretti nodded. "Okay, Major, we're in the eye of a thunderstorm, doesn't worry us a bit."

The plane was the new development based on the English Electric Canberra, not much faster than the original (its maximum speed at 35,000 feet was still only 780 m.p.h.), but with its integral wing fuel tanks its range was a very satisfactory 3,630 miles, and the Colonel had said, frowning: "Well, the plane's got to get back home again, hasn't it? Unless we dump it, with Moretti, in the middle of the Atlantic Ocean."

Bramble looked at the pale blue glow of the altimeter: 32,360 feet. It was black out there, and he said: "Black as the pit from pole to pole . . . Eighty-five minutes to go, and we're going to be cut out of it by then?"

"Keep your fingers crossed, Bram. You just might have to jump in the middle of it, won't that be fun? All that directional work to worry about, too."

He was secretly gloating. His orders were to drop them at five thousand four hundred feet, the engines off, and he laughed and said: "That's a terrible long way to fall, but if we let you out any lower I can't start my engines up over water. The Colonel insisted that I overfly Angola in silence, and I'm going to need all the height I can get."

Bramble said sourly: "Make it ten thousand as far as I'm concerned, a long free fall never hurt anybody, especially when you're as fond of it as I am."

"No sir. Fifty-four hundred, or the Colonel will have my guts for garters."

He went back into the cabin where the others were waiting. There were five of them there in the plane's belly. Edgars Jefferson, the Chicago Negro who had been thrown out of Vietnam for a mutiny that the Major considered was wholly justified, was intently studying his Swahili grammar. There was Efrem Collas, the Israeli, catching up on his sleep with his feet up in Jefferson's lap. There was Sergeant Roberts, who was passing round a bottle of the "Staff Irish," as he called it, the Colonel's favorite Irish whisky; and Hamash the Turk, who had become very close friends with Cass Fragonard (down there below them somewhere) ever since he had lost a foot in the Dead Sea that time they had to blow up an Arab guerilla submarine. (He had told Cass, enjoying the joke: "Okay, you've got two tin legs, and I've only got one, but give me

35

a year or so and I'll catch up.") And finally, there was Rudi Vicek, who ran Communications, a technological wizard who had escaped from behind the Iron Curtain four years ago.

Every spare inch of the plane's belly was crowded with the containers, their parachutes ready attached; they would open automatically at four hundred and fifty feet.

Edgars Jefferson looked up as Bramble came in and said: "Man, if my ancestors really spoke Swahili, they must have been pretty damn simple people; it's a pretty damn simple language, did you know that?"

"You'd better know it well," Bramble said. "You've got a tough job ahead of you."

"Well . . ." Edgars grinned. "I studied it back in Chicago, racial pride, all that crap. I'll manage. Just a little brushing up is all."

He had volunteered, Edgars, to infiltrate into General Guevara Lincoln's army—if, and when, they found him.

Moretti's voice came over the intercom, booming at them from the speaker: "I've picked up the signal, Major, if you want to take it. Three minutes to go, and we're dropping down."

The sudden silence as the engines were cut was oppressive, and he felt a tightening in the pit of his stomach as the great plane seemed to slide down, lower, lower, sickeningly fast.

Efrem Collas had leaped to his feet and was unfastening the hatch in the floor. The green light came on and Bramble eased his bulk into the opening, sitting on the floor with his legs dangling in space, his hands gripping tightly. The wind was rushing up at them. He adjusted his padded helmet and said: "Fast as you can, free fall to five hundred, keep your finders on and glide right on down, onto the signal. I want to see everybody land right on top of that box. They're supposed to get the containers, but we may as well give them a hand. . . ."

He was thinking: Christ, a free fall of three thousand nine hundred feet, I'll never make it.

He switched on the tiny box at his chest and heard its

friendly *beep-beep-beep* that meant they were in range, and kept his eyes glued on the light.

It went red, and he pushed with his hands and thrust himself out into the cold air. He held out his arms and legs and floated down, and saw Sergeant Roberts, the expert, closing in on him, arms outstretched. They held hands as Hamash came into the circle, and he looked and saw that Vicek had thrust out the bundles and was following them. It was strange to see the plane sweeping away and not to hear it; Moretti would not restart his motors till he was clear of Angolan skies and over the water, gliding gently and in silence out to the Atlantic Ocean, skimming over the waves.

Edgars Jefferson was a little behind them, and they slid sideways to join him and link hands, and Collas went past them fast and arrested his speed with outflung limbs. In a moment they caught up with him, and now they were all together, all except Vicek, who was above them and a hundred feet to the side.

Sergeant Roberts yelled out at him: "Dive in, you stupid son of a bitch, you can make it; you want to spoil a nice party?"

Vicek swung his body over, brought his arms and his legs in to his side, and almost exploded among them, and as Roberts grabbed him, he said: "Not bad, Rudi, but watch my stomach—I got a hernia."

There were the six of them together now, a perfect circle, and Bramble yelled: "Break it up, ten seconds to open!"

They pushed themselves free, and the altitude checks on the parachutes flopped them out. Bramble twisted round and caught hold of a line and pulled hard, sliding to one side where the beeper told him to go, and when he hit the ground, very gently, and rolled over onto his back and hauled in the lines, the loud sound at his chest told him he was right on top of the box.

He scrambled to his feet, and Paul was there with his party, shaking his hand and saying: "Nice drop, boys and

37

girls, right on pinpoint," and Bramble grinned an said: "My favorite sport, Paul; it's exhilarating."

Paul knew, of course. He said: "Bad quicksand right behind you, forest and swamp on two sides, the mountain ahead of us. Betty was right. We couldn't have found a better spot if we'd searched for a year."

The others had landed, not one of them more than twenty feet from his neighbor, and had slipped out of their harnesses and were rolling up the chutes for disposal.

Cass was there, thumping Hamash on the back and saying: "How did the tin foot hold out, you terrible Turk?"

Aklilu and Drima had their arms full of parachutes, and were striding with them to the edge of the quicksand and throwing them in. The others gathered up the containers and piled them ready for porterage, and Paul said: "A couple of hours from here to the top, that's going to be our H.Q. I want two men to stay behind till daylight to make sure there's nothing left lying around. Aklilu and Efrem Collas, okay? Come up to us as soon as you've made a thorough check. No footprints, and no damn great parachutes lying on top of the quicksand."

Under the bright light of the moon the shadows of the umbrella thorns were deep, deep purple. The night was quiet, a faint breeze blowing, warm and sticky. In the distance, they could hear the thunder of hooves on the hard sand; a herd of zebra among the rocks? There was the savage shriek of a hyena, and then all was silent again.

Paul took Bramble's arm and led him under the trees, and said: "Here, this is where the glider comes in when we're ready for it. You'll have to take a look at it in the morning, but tonight we'll rest up for a couple of hours. What's the news of Rick Meyers?"

"On his way here," Bramble said. "He flew into Luso in Angola, on an ordinary Portuguese Airlines plane. That's only two hundred and forty miles from here. He's getting a truck, and his trip here ought to take him right past General Lincoln's territory—or at least where we think Lincoln is. Information so far is pretty sketchy, but he's quite confident he'll be able to find out all he wants to know. You can't hide an army of eight thousand men.

38

Eight thousand, and growing all the time. The best bet is that they're camped somewhere along the Kasai River, which marks the Angolan border. And he'll be on this side of it, without a doubt."

"How sure is that bet?"

Bramble shrugged. "The Colonel came up with some Intelligence from the Angolan army. No time yet to evaluate its accuracy, but the old man says accept it for the time being, so that's what we'll do till we hear from Rick."

"And Dogger?"

"Dogger," Bramble said, "is a lot easier. You just follow a trail of blood." He looked at Paul curiously. "Did you know we had a man in Zambia?"

"Not Zambia. Central Africa in general. Yes, I know about that. You just might meet him. Except that it's not a him, it's a her."

"Oh, really? Well, anyway . . . Communications were buzzing all day long yesterday, and it seems that Dogger has crashed through the Zambian border, literally *crashed* through. He destroyed the Zambian military post there, murdered everyone in it, burned it to the ground, and moved on. He wiped out three villages in forty-eight hours, no one knows why, all on his line of march. At six o'clock yesterday morning he was at the Manyinga River, making rafts for the crossing."

Paul pulled the map from his hip pocket and took out the pen-light. "Give me the names of those villages, Bram."

"Serimoji, Klumanana, and Omesi."

"And whereabouts on the river?"

"Twelve miles from its confluence with the Kabompo."

Paul studied the map intently. In a little while: "Then he's moving on a fairly constant course, about two hundred and ninety-five degrees. He's thirty miles inside Kamapa already and heading for—I'd say the diamond fields. Would that make sense?"

"Yes, it would. He's got seven or eight thousand Africans with him, and they'll present no problem; all he's got to do is feed them and keep them half drunk. But he's also got sixty or seventy Europeans and Americans with him, and that's a different question altogether. Czechs, Spaniards, South Africans, Germans, Dutch, Greeks, even a couple of Bulgarians. They're all professional soldiers of fortune, and if he doesn't give them something to put in their pockets once in a while, they'll desert him, and he's bright enough to know that. A good raid on a diamond field would be a highly intelligent move, would consolidate his forces for the big showdown with Guevara Lincoln."

"Arms?"

"Our man in Zambia—our woman—says mostly machine guns and rifles. An enormous amount of ammunition, apparently." He said drily: "American arms, hijacked from the Military Assistance Mission to Congo three months ago. But he's also got seven pieces of field artillery, a British 25-pound gun-howitzer, four German Nebelwerfers, and two U.S. 75mm. recoilless guns. A considerable, though undetermined number of mortars . . ."

Paul said sharply: "Nebelwerfers?"

"That's right. Shell loadings changed from chemical to high explosive and incendiary. He's been using incendiary shells most of the time, doing terrible damage."

"I see. Then we'll have to spike them, won't we? What's he moving them with? Half-tracks? Three-quarter trucks?"

"No. Ordinary ten-ton trucks."

"And he's still covering forty miles a day and slicing his way through everything. My respect for his competence is increasing. We've got to swing him north a bit more, haven't we?"

"And that's not going to be easy."

Paul grinned. "I put it up to Cass. I think that when Cass lost his legs, all the life from them went to his brain. He said: 'Tell me where you want him, *mon Commmmandant*, and I will personally see that he goes there.' And he'll do it."

Bramble looked around him. The dark shapes of the tall umbrella trees were specters hanging over their heads. He said: "A good place for the glider. Is Cass going alone?"

"Hamash to back him up."

"Communications?"

"Sensors, nothing else. He'll have three of the Mark

40

Sevens, placed at strategic intervals, dropped in the sand where he can get to them. Anything else would be too dangerous. Rudy Vicek is setting it up now."

"Dogger won't accept Cass Fragonard very easily."

"I know that," he said quietly. "Cass knows it too. I take it we don't know the precise number of Dogger's Europeans?"

Bramble said again: "Sixty or seventy. They're the backbone of his army. And they're a pretty murderous lot of cutthroats. But good soldiers, all of them." He was wondering how hard he could push. He looked at Paul obliquely and said. "Who's the woman in Zambia? Or am I being indiscreet?"

"Indiscreet, no. But the old man doesn't tell me everything." He sighed. "Not nearly enough, I sometimes think. She calls herself Tunisia. Leila Tunisia. Apparently she's half French, half Arab, half Greek, half English, and half Spanish."

"That's a lot of halves."

"And I'm told she's a lot of woman. Maybe we'll find out, who knows? She works, ostensibly, for an Algerian trading company that has offices all over Africa. A good cover."

Efrem Collas was approaching them, gliding in in silence, wiping at the sweat on the back of his neck. He said: "Everything out of sight, Major."

"Good. Stay here with Aklilu till daylight for a final check."

"Will do." He melted away into the shadows, and Paul said: "What about the overflights?"

"Ah, yes, it all hinges on that, doesn't it. Well . . ." Bramble took a deep breath. "The Cuanza Air Prospecting Service, operating out of Carvalha Airport in Angola, has been working for the CIA, apparently, until just recently when Washington decided they were rocking the boat too much and withdrew their support. The Colonel stepped in and hired them for a mineral survey in the border areas, and persuaded them to take Moretti on as his personal pilot. They've got a nice little Breguet 1050 Alizé, a pretty slow plane, but a nice range, a single Dart turboprop. The

Colonel's practically bought it from them. Hell, he's practically bought the whole damn company, and Moretti will keep up a constant patrol over the area. If he has to stray too far—well, the boundaries are not very well marked, are they? And if he runs into trouble, all he has to do is dive to nought feet and head for the border; in Angola he's legal."

"Good. And if your men are ready, we'll head for H.Q. Plan 'A' starts tomorrow at sun-up." He hoisted a heavy container onto his shoulder.

Struggling under their loads, the silent column, an advance guard of nine men from Colonel Tobin's Private Army, began the long, painful haul to the top of the cliff.

When the sun came up, the land was a shimmering panorama around them.

They had reached the peak itself now and were staring out to the southeast, where the land rolled on and on and on to the borders of Zambia.

A great wide plain of hard sand lay below them, on which a thousand giant boulders lay, incredibly round, like enormous footballs of solid rock which had been rolled there by a gargantuan hand a million years ago, for three or four miles before coming to a halt.

Interspersed among them, where the water lay, there were great patches of dark forest, and in the dryer parts the huge baobab trees, with their stubby boles and stunted branches, stood like grotesquely inverted vegetables.

To their right, the mountain descended in gentle rills, heavily forested, the creepers festooning the trees and making a solid wall of impenetrable growth. A thin ribbon of waterfall was sending its spray high into the air, and five elephants, a bull, two females and two calves, were wandering slowly across the grass. Beyond them the sky was dark with thunderclouds, and Bramble said: "We flew through that lot last night; it scared the wits out of me."

Paul sat on a flat-topped slab of columnar basalt, a natural armchair, stretched out his long legs and said: "Rick Meyers, when do you think we can expect him?"

"A day or two. Three or four at the most."

"By which time Cass and Hamash ought to be on their way."

"Oh yes, I should think so."

"What about Edgars Jefferson? He's got the hardest job of the lot, is he up to it?"

"Yes, most certainly."

"He'll never pass for a Swahili-speaking native."

"He doesn't have to, as long as he has enough of the language to communicate. His story will be that he was brought up in Liberia, so English is his natural tongue. His French is fairly good, and his Swahili is fluent enough for him to say he's traveled all over Africa, west to east, looking for trouble. He'll say he worked as a docker in Monrovia, got put in jail there three years ago, escaped, and has been criss-crossing the continent ever since. Rick Meyers decided he shouldn't have too firm a cover, so that he can't be pinned down so easily."

"Well, if Rick's satisfied, then I am. You'd better spend the next three or four days plotting the terrain. This is where we're going to have to fight and I want to know every inch of it."

"We'll be ready when the time comes." The sweat was running down his back as he manhandled his load up the hill. The nighttime monkeys were screeching all around them now. He said, musing: "When the time comes . . . Dogger versus General Lincoln. Two pains in the arse at each other's throats, am I getting my anatomy mixed up? I wonder which of the two is the more deadly?"

"When the battle begins," Paul said, "that's when we'll find that out."

They moved on slowly, in the humid, windless, African night.

CHAPTER FIVE

THE LUNGWEBUNGU RIVER
CO-ORDINATES: 22.18E
13.19S

He was tall and thin and immensely strong, and he wore a sharp, pointed beard, a drooping moustache and his hair in an Afro cut, though no one would have mistaken him for an African.

He had taken off his uniform jacket to have it pressed—he was very fussy about his uniform, even when he was fighting—and his T-shirt, dyed dark green, was brightly patterned in colored silks, embroidered by the women the chiefs had brought for him. He wore black patent leather shoes, and he carried a beautiful Malacca cane with a carved ivory head to it; he didn't often draw it, but it was a sword-stick, made in Lisbon for the Portuguese Commander of the Seventh Artillery and taken from him when he had been murdered.

He was pacing up and down outside his tent, his tight khaki trousers immaculately creased, the black belt decorated with silver coins; his bare arms were formidable, the biceps rippling. Behind him, his body naked and bloodied, a young African from the Odena tribe was tied by the wrists to two bent saplings that had pulled him half off the ground so that he hung there as though crucified. The leather thongs round his wrists were cutting deeply into them, and the ants had found the wounds.

The young man's front teeth had all been broken, and it was hard for him to speak, but he said, insisting: "I've told you the truth, General, the truth; I didn't see anything at all; I was in the fields, all the time. When I came back my village was burned; there was no one left alive."

General Lincoln turned back. He said coldly: "Your village, Serimoji."

"Yes sir. General. Serimoji. Just a small village, thirty, thirty-five families. But I was . . . in the field, cutting . . . cutting the flax."

The clearing was darkly framed by the trees, so densely packed that the sky was blotted out, and it was marked by a circle of small fires attended by the sentries, those of them who were on the ground; the others were high in the branches, listening for alien sounds over the distant washing of the cataracts on the river.

During the night the young man had been found by one of the river's smaller tributaries, hiding his canoe, covering it over with ferns, and he had been seized by the General's scouts and dragged into the camp.

The beatings had been routine, but now . . . now he knew that he was going to die, and there was nothing in the world he craved more than an hour or two left to live.

The General said: "But you heard the shooting?"

"Yes, sir. I was afraid . . . I hid . . ."

"The shooting of cannon?"

"Yes, sir."

"I want to know what kind of cannon. What's your name?"

"Rumaki, General. My father was . . ."

"I don't care to hear about your father. You're a long way from Serimoji now. How did you get here?"

"By river, General; it's easy, the stream runs fast . . . my canoe . . ." The saplings, under tension, were pulling his wrists off slowly, and he fainted with the pain of it, and when he came to his senses again, the General was closer, peering into his face, lifting up an eyelid.

The soldiers were still there, gathered round in an untidy circle, still holding their submachine guns at the ready.

But another man was there too, an old and sly and gnarled African in the ceremonial robe of the Hondiri tribe, a chief, perhaps even a paramount chief, and the General was saying to him: "Well, am I gonna kill this boy or not, man?"

There was a wicked, malevolent grin on the old man's face; there were tufts of wiry white hair at his chin, and the eyes were deep-sunk in black parchment that looked

46

like ancient goatskin, improperly cured. He was shaking his head.

"Why you kill him, General? Let the enemy kill him. He can fight for us, another man."

"He don't have no guts, man, you heard him. I don't need no crap like that working for me."

"No, perhaps not. As you think."

"Give me your sword."

The old chief pulled the long curved sword he was carrying from its cracked red leather scabbard, an old Portuguese naval saber, handed it to the General, and the General laid the Malacca cane on the ground, and rested the sharp edge of the sword on the young man's upper arm, sawing it back and forth, very gently. He said: "You got one more chance to tell me, boy."

The young man squirmed. "I've told you, General sir, everything I know. Please . . . please don't kill me. I fight for you, I promise."

"How many cannons? What kind of cannon?"

"No sir, I don't know, sir, I never saw . . ." The ants were biting him now where the blood had gathered between his legs, and he heard the General say: "I think you're a spy for that white devil Dogger, you know that? A spy."

"No sir, General, I swear it."

"You like the white man, don't you, boy?"

"No sir, I don't have anything to do with them. . . ."

"A Kamapan from Serimoji—why, don't you know all your people? They bring white men in to run their railways, they bring white men in to build their bridges, they even give their diamonds to the white men to pay for guns to shoot down blacks with, didn't you know that?"

The coma was coming over him again, and he barely saw the sword go up. He felt no pain, but he heard the swish as the young tree took his arm up high among the branches, and then the second, and he fell to the ground and rolled over, suddenly conscious that both his arms were gone.

He heard the General say, the voice coming and going now, fading into great distance and coming back again:

"Take him out into the jungle for the hyenas and the buzzards to finish off."

Then all the pain was gone, and the coma was over him, and he did not feel it when someone lifted up his ankles and dragged him away, nor know that he was being thrown into a deep gully where the fast-running white water was turning red with the blood that poured out of him. And before the man had gone back to the camp, he was dead.

A young girl was bringing the General his jacket, helping him on with it, pleased with the honor he was giving her, but he ignored her and said to one of the soldiers: "Get the chiefs, all of them. Now. My chair."

One of the men hurried to bring the teakwood and ebony chair, and the General sat in it and waited till someone put a stool under his feet and someone else brought him a bottle of beer; and then the chiefs were coming in and squatting in a semicircle round him, sitting on their heels on the green moss floor of the jungle, tucking their ochre robes delicately between their thighs, holding their rifles upthrust in front of them. One of them clicked his tongue and moved away from the dripping blood, still spilling down from a severed arm in the tops of the trees.

There were fourteen of them, and four interpreters. They had no common language, these people, and everything that went on among them was translated two, three, sometimes four times, till it was quite sure that every one of them knew what was going on. There was no waiting; they all spoke at once, each preoccupied with his own ideas, each trying, at the same time, to absorb the ideas of their leader, the man they knew as General Guevara Lincoln.

They all wore khaki uniforms, but most of them still affected parts, at least, of their old tribal costumes; some wore animal skins draped over their shoulders, some carried flowing plumes on their heads, and others wore the ornate necklaces of bone and water-buck horn that meant they belonged to the river tribes.

The General tossed away the empty beer bottle, wiped the froth from his mouth with the back of his hand, and

48

said: "Man, there ain't one of you here that looks to me like a soldier." He sighed. "Abu-Subu, they tell me your whole tribe is joining us, is that true?"

Abu-Subu was chief of the Subusus, a tough and expert jungle fighter who had been heading the abortive revolt against the Portuguese just a few miles from here, back over the Angolan border. An old-fashioned man, he still wore the leopards' teeth and claws round his neck that signified he was one of the warrior class, and the elephant-hair band around his wrist with purple cloth that indicated he was of royal blood. Even though he had personally killed his father, the late king, with his own hands, he still considered the bonds of royalty to be binding.

He said stolidly: "All of them, General. The number of warriors is ten times ten. Four tens of them have rifles, the others only their spears and their knives and their bows. But they can all use rifles."

"Then we'll see that they get them. Tonight, when the supply column comes in, have thirty of your men there . . ." He corrected himself, remembering: "Have three tens of them there to carry away the guns."

"It will be."

The General looked over at the chiefs, studying their faces, searching out their loyalties. He said: "Tonight, before the moon comes up, the big ship from the port brings us guns, more guns than a man can count. I want three tens of men from each tribe, together with the oldest sons of all the chiefs, and I want them to be at the river, no man drunk, to see that every warrior in the army has a rifle, and as many bullets as he can carry and as many bullets as his women can carry. There is enough for all, and if there is not enough, I will get more. I have promised you, and I will get more."

There was a murmur of approval, then the General raised his voice suddenly and said: "The white man must be killed."

Instantly, one of the interpreters sprang to his feet, lifted his arms out wide, and shouted: *"O branbran usa fi-a'kri!"*

He shouted it out again, louder, and began to clap his

hands to the rhythm, and they all took up the chant, clapping their hands too: *"O branbran usa fi-a'kri, o branbran usa fi-a'kri . . !"* Those among them who were more sophisticated, and could speak the General's own language, shouted the phrase in English, and some of them took the single word, kill, *a'kri*, and shouted it out in a kind of counterpoint.

Three of the younger chiefs leaped up and began to dance, stomping their great splayed feet into the moss, holding their rifles high, the sweat pouring down their bodies, and the seated assembly kept up the chant till, it seemed, the whole jungle was resounding with their anger.

Only the General was silent. His dark eyes were cold and impassive as he watched them, and when he judged that they were excited enough he held up his hands for silence.

In a little while the sound died down, and he said:

"We welcome the new warriors of the Subusus. *A'kri, a'kri!*"

They shouted back at him: *"A'kri, a'kri, a'kri!"*

He called for silence again and said: "When they have taken the oath, they will march beside us to Ngaru." He waited to let the name sink in, and then said, more quietly: "I have decided that we will go to Mount Ngaru and seek out the white man there. Who among you remembers his name?"

It was Abu-Subu who shouted back: "Dogger, *a'kri*, Dogger, *a'kri!*" and the General nodded his approval and said:

"Be sure you all remember it. Dogger, Dogger, Dogger, a white devil who must be killed. The man who kills him will sit beside me when I am ruler, and he shall have all the *tembe* he can drink, and all the virgins he can take, and his name shall be inscribed in his tribal lore for all men to remember. It is this man, Dogger, who is the enemy, and all the white men who fight with him. I have spoken to my God, and He has promised me that the white man's bullets will turn to water and that we shall conquer! Now go, all of you, and tell your men that tomorrow we march for Mount Ngaru. Each chief will send

50

his own scouts ahead, in the way they have always done, and the scouts will bring back news to me, and I will decide when we strike. The scouts will move in silence, and the tribes will move in silence, and the chiefs will remember that the day is near when the last white man will be driven from Africa, and the land will be once again the land of our tribal fathers. Go now. Go now and alert your men. Tomorrow, we move."

He threw back his head suddenly and laughed out loud, his strong white teeth gleaming. He said: "Today, this little place is ours, the jungle, the river, the trees and all the birds and animals in it. Tomorrow . . ."

He waited a moment, and then, his voice a shriek: "Tomorrow, the whole of Africa!"

The din was appalling. The chiefs were shouting, the interpreters were trying to make themselves heard, and even the soldiers were yelling encouragement at each other. The General waited a few moments, and then snatched a machine gun from one of the sentries and fired a burst into the air, and in the sudden silence, he said angrily: "Did you not hear me! I said go now!"

Quieter now, reproaching themselves, the chiefs moved back into the forest. The trees gathered around them as they went to their camps along the edge of the river, where the cataracts threw their fine wet spray and made a swamp of the ground. They moved in absolute silence, not even the rustling of the humus marking their going.

Only one man remained behind, rising lazily to his feet and finding a more comfortable seat on a smooth, flat stone. The General looked at him and smiled slowly, and said: "Well, Abdul Karan?"

Abdul Karan's face was smooth and chubby, and he wore steel-rimmed glasses and was dressed in a khaki uniform. He was a plump, affable man in his early forties, and had been a lecturer in modern languages, and a Doctor of Philosophy at the University of Khartoum before moving to Cairo as anchorman for the Libyan junta which had seized power two years previously. He was a Sudanese, widely traveled, and had spent the last six months with the rebels in Chad, coaching them in the guerrilla tactics he had learned first in Moscow, and then—when the Russians had become disenchanted with him—in Peking. And on his return to the Sudan, he had personally and happily headed the group of underground right-wingers that was systematically destroying the local Communist Party.

Now he had found a man he could follow for the rest of his days.

He said, beaming: "Guevara, you're a born leader. You know just the right moment to play the fool. You're not really going to fight him on Mount Ngaru, are you?"

The General laughed: "Of course not! Ngaru's a trap, only one way in and one way out, a dead man's gulch. No, that's not for me. But that sonofabitch Dogger's got a pretty good Intelligence service, and I want him to think that's where I'm heading. Like that, we bottle him up there, instead of him—us."

"Someone you don't trust?"

"I don't trust nobody. You gonna tell me with eight thousand savages we don't have a single one of them working for Dogger? You really believe that?"

The Sudanese nodded. "You're right, of course."

"Logistics, Abdul Karan. Dogger's supplies come up from the south; I want him to get too far ahead of them, stretch his lines of communication a little further. Given time, we can get every villager in Kamapa on our side, and by Christ, we'll outnumber him two to one."

"And if they don't join us? The Kamapans?"

The General said drily: "The ones that want to live will. They're either for us, or against us. I don't care if I have to wipe out half the population, just so I get the other half on my side."

"That might not be the best way to do it."

"No? You been reading too many books. Abdul. The Kamapans are a backward people, they still think whitey's going to help them out of their troubles; we've got to teach them a lesson, bring them round to more progressive thinking. I care if only ten percent of them is left when I get through—I tell you, that ten percent's going to be on our side. And you know something? Dogger's got the same

52

idea—why do you think he's *burning* his way through? I'll tell you why. Because when he's good and ready it'll be: Fight with me, or get burned up the way them others did. That's exactly how it is with Dogger."

"Maybe."

"You bet your ass it is. You want a beer?"

He clapped his hands and the young girl who had helped him with his uniform came out of the tent. He reached out and touched her, very gently, and said: "Bring beer," and when she had gone back into the tent, he looked at Abdul Karan and said: "She's a good kid, hotter'n hell. Her father's Dakiru—came in with three hundred men, tough sonsofbitches from the mountains up north. You know Dakiru?"

Abdul Karan nodded: "I know him. And with Dakiru on our side, we've got three more sub-tribes ready to join us. It's axiomatic; wherever Dakiru goes, they go. What about Dogger's heavy guns?"

"Yes, the guns." The General scowled. "How did he get them howitzers over the mountain?"

"A certain ingenuity. He's no fool, Dogger."

"He ain't no Alexander, either. His thinking's all wrong, did you know that?"

Abdul Karan raised an eyebrow and said nothing, and the General went on: "You know why he wants to fight me? I'll tell you why. He knows the Angolan army has been giving us a bad time, keeping our heads way down, and he knows that now every tribesman for a hundred thousand miles around is coming to join us, so he figures to hit me before I get too big. But he's too late, friend. He shoulda stopped me at the border. Pretty damn soon we'll be too big to get stopped by *anyone*, and you know something? Dogger thinks that because he's white, he's a better soldier than I am. Ha! Maybe if he compares himself to the bunch of savages he's been up against so far, he's right. But he's up against me, now, and he still doesn't know I'm a better man than he is. I put my faith in the sword, Abdul, in my own right arm. He puts his in his color. Now what kind of crap is that?"

"You have to do something about those guns. He'll slaughter your men."

"Yeah. Yeah." He thought for a while, and said: "All his major battles, they've been during daylight. He's not a night fighter. Maybe we should hit him in the dark; he doesn't seem to like it."

Abdul Karan shook his head. "No, that's not true. He broke out of a trap in Biafra during the night, wiped out two regiments of the Nigerian army while he was about it, and captured seven tanks and twelve half-tracks. He hit a Zambian column that had been sent to wipe him out, also at night, and killed every man jack of them. He can fight at night if he has to."

"It's those goddam Europeans . . . If we could separate them from his Africans, we'd walk right over them."

"Of course. But that's a mighty big if, Guevara."

The General swore softly. "There's got to be a way. We've got *right* on our side, that's got to count for something."

"Historically, it never has."

The General said sarcastically: "For a man who went to college, you don't have no brains at all, Abdul. What about the French Revolution? Seventeen eighty-nine."

Abdul Karan said quickly: "The peasants had all the right in the world on their side, and they got nowhere until the army joined them. And maybe that's your answer."

"Huh?"

"The Kamapan army. They're good fighters, but badly equipped and badly paid. A high rate of desertion. So figure out a way to get them on our side; it'll turn the balance."

The General said: "No. The Kamapa people have got this . . . nationalist thing going for them. They'll never take orders from an outsider . . ."

As Abdul Karan began to protest, he raised a hand and said: "Yeah, I know. We can use them against the Zambians, and against the Angolans, and they'll love it. But that means we have to hit Dogger first, get him off our backs before the main course is open, before the pattern starts to shape itself. We hit Dogger, we wipe him out, we take over

54

the diamond fields, and we use the money to bring over the Kamapa army. Then, and not before then, we can move on. Anyone who stands in our way, we'll wipe them out. We'll use Kamapans against the Zambians, Zambians against the Kamapans; it's the only thing that makes sense."

"A lot of people are going to get killed."

"Yeah, I know that." He was sullen now, brooding. He said: "I don't like it any more than you do, Abdul, but to cut a canker, you have to be prepared to hurt. Okay, tomorrow there'll be half a million Africans dead, but I'm not worrying about tomorrow. I'm thinking of your kids and mine a couple of generations from now. By the time I'm a granddaddy I don't want to see a white man in Africa, and that means that anyone that's dealing with them now, talking with them, any kind of a dialogue with the white devils, they've got to be wiped out too . . ."

Abdul Karan said drily: "You're out of character now. You don't have to call them white devils for my benefit, I'm a college man, remember?"

The General stared at him, not at all pleased. He said at last: "You don't really hate them the way I do, do you?"

"No."

"Not even after what they did to your country?"

"My country was better off under the British than it is now, under the Egyptians."

"So?" His voice was hard.

Abdul Karan laughed: "But I agree with the intellectual argument. A continent without a single white man . . . oh, maybe a few—houseboys, water-carriers, that sort of thing . . . but one hundred percent black. It's a concept to turn a man's mind. I don't think we'll ever see it, but I'm prepared to fight for it because fighting's the thing I'm best at. I used to study literature in Cairo, till I discovered I liked slitting Egyptian throats better. So, we're soul brothers, Guevara. And you need me, don't ever forget that."

"I need you?"

"Yes, you do. And you know what else you need?"

"I'm listening, man."

"I hate to say it, I really do, but you need a depopu-

55

lated Kamapa. Sure, part of the army we can use, they wouldn't be soldiers if they weren't a little dishonest. But the rest . . . When you march on, Guevara, you've got to have *no one* behind you who can rally round to the old concept, to the idea that it needs the white man's genius to run Africa. That's the Kamapans' real hang-up, isn't it? Everybody out of step except them. They're the ones who are holding that dialogue you were talking about. And that means a depopulated Kamapa." He said it again: "Depopulated."

The General took a long, deep breath. "What's the population figure, Abdul."

"A million and a half. A high percentage of women, about eight hundred thousand males. Half of them too old or too young to fight, and we're down to four hundred thousand already. Twenty percent of those are in the army, and we can use them, and let's say that half the remainder will come over to us. That leaves a net figure of a hundred and sixty thousand civilians of fighting age, scattered over the whole damn territory. Not much of a problem, is it?"

"And not much of a price to pay, either."

"A dream's worth any price you want to put on it, Guevara."

"Well, figure out, for Christ's sake, what to do about those heavy guns."

Abdul Karan got to his feet and brushed the clinging moss off his trousers. "Give me a day or two, I'll tell you exactly what to do. By the time you reach the Mwombejhi River, I'll have the answer for you."

"The Mwombejhi?" The General stared at him.

"Yes. That's where you have to hit Major Dogger. You can throw ten thousand carcasses into the water if you attack him there. He'll be crossing it in about four days' time."

The General was silent. Abdul Karan waited a little while, and said: "Well, I'm going to turn in. See you in the morning."

General Lincoln said again: "The Mwombejhi. Yes, I

see what you mean. All right, we'll leave at sun-up. You got a woman to sleep with?"

"Yes."

"You're a good man, Abdul. See you at five o'clock."

He turned on his heel and ducked into his tent. The young girl was waiting for him there. She undressed him carefully, then slipped out of her shift and lay down beside him on the straw-stuffed mattress. He reached back and flung the tent's awning closed, then curled his body round hers and waited for the distant hooting from the river that would tell him supplies were on their way.

It's always logistics, he thought. In Africa, it's the man who can keep his army supplied that wins in the end. He was thinking: If only I can get behind Dogger and cut him off from his supplies . . .

CHAPTER SIX

BUSANGA KNOLL
CO-ORDINATES: 24.12E
                13.13S

There were ten, twelve, fifteen weaver birds' nests among the spikes of the thorny acacia, and they looked like handfuls of yellow straw tucked in among the green branches.

The knoll rose incongruously out of the swampland, a dry, burnt-umber patch of land a couple of miles across that seemed to have pushed its way up out of the stinking wet mud of the flats around it, as though the land below the swamp were dusty-dry, as though this particular hill had exploded out of the water in its search for the hot sun.

Only a hundred feet away, the black water's edge was alive with crocodile; up here, a solitary gerenuk was standing on its hind legs and feasting off the lower twigs and shoots of the huge tree.

Beyond the tree, at the top of the rise, Cass Fragonard was lying on his belly, a thorn bush pulled across him, and he was staring out at the plain that lay ahead, the glasses at his eyes. Beside him Hamash the Turk was refilling the water bottles from a tiny spring of clear water that bubbled out of the sand and ran back down into the swamp.

They had seen the dust of the truck a long time ago; now the dust had gone, and they knew that it had moved off the sand and onto the grasses. It was steady in the binoculars now, an old three-ton Chevy with spare tires roped all over its sides, no less than eight of them on the side that Cass could see now. The canvas tarp was flapping, and he fancied he caught the glint of aluminum, of pots and pans inside.

He said: "A trader, piled high with *cassoulets à pieds.*"

Hamash laughed. "Maybe we can put him to use. Your old tin legs are tired, so maybe he can find a couple of new ones for you." He screwed on the tops of the bottles firmly, and splashed water over his face. The sun was roasting them, broiling, a bed of hot charcoal over their heads. He squinted down at the truck and said: "And now, you tell me why he left the sand and hit the moss. There's no track down there, he could have kept going on the hard sand, it's easier."

"*Oui, c'est ça.* And it makes more dust too."

"Then what's he hiding from? One of Dogger's men?"

"*Pas encore, mon Dieu.* If Dogger's as far west as this, we're all in trouble." Cass laughed softly. "He's got a flat, another one."

The truck had stopped, and the driver had climbed down to stare at the front wheel. They fancied they could hear him cursing, and as he straightened up, Cass suddenly said: "*Mon Dieu!*" He handed the glasses to Hamash, grinning, and said: "Take a look, *mon vieux.*"

Hamash had clambered into a crouch and was bent double under a mass of brilliant orange flame-lilies, the plant that had guided them to the clear water here. An Isabella chameleon, blue and orange, was curled up in among its foliage, immobile. Hamash shook his head. "I don't need the glasses, they're for old men, especially old Frenchmen. I see him."

"Rick Meyers. By God, Captain Meyers. Let's go down and help him with that wheel."

"Two miles," Hamash said. "If we time it right, he'll just have finished by the time we get there. So let's go, a nice, slow walk. One thing to do first, though, just in case he's out of contact."

"Out of contact? Rick Meyers? You're out of your mind, you stupid Turk."

But Hamash squatted on his heels in the shadow of the lilies and switched on his R-phone. He said: "Come in, Orange, this is Apricot, do you read me?"

The tiny receiver was plugged into his ear, and the voice said: "Go ahead, Apricot, you're beautiful. And give me your co-ordinates." It was Rudi Vicek, far away on the summit of Mount Ngaru, playing with his beloved radio-phones, micro-miniaturized to the point where a console the size of a cigar box could pick up twelve independent broadcasts from as far as a hundred and eight miles.

Hamash was rapidly unfolding the map, and he ran a black-haired finger over it and said: "Co-ordinates twenty-four twelve and thirteen thirteen. . . ."

"You've made good time. . . ."

"And Trader Vic is down there, two miles on two-eight-five, a flat tire."

"Hold on, Apricot." The set went dead, and in a moment it was Paul's voice at the other end: "Apricot? How's it going out there?"

"It's going pretty damn good. You know about Trader Vic"

"We know. He had to make a wide detour to get round the forest."

"And we had to get around the swamp. We're going down to say hello, all right?"

"Good, we'll tell him you're coming. Anything else?"

"Not yet."

"Out then. Keep in touch."

Hamash switched off and took a sip of the water, cupping it in his hand so as not to take even a drop from the fresh filled bottles. He hitched his heavy pack onto his back, and set off down the slope toward the valley.

Cass wondered for a moment if he should leave his load behind and retrieve it later, but he thought: That bastard—where does he get off, calling me an old man? He thumped Hamash playfully on the shoulder, nearly sending him sprawling, and growled: "If you're getting tired, I'll carry your backpack for you."

Rick Meyers was standing by the truck now, staring up at them through his own binoculars, waving a cheerful hand, and they saw him lugging out the jack and getting the wheel off, and thirty minutes later he was letting the axle down again and then turning to meet them, his hand outstretched.

He said: "Good to see you, Cass, Hamash. Aren't you a bit off course?"

61

Cass grimaced. *"Un petit peu.* You too, Rick. We thought we'd give you a hand with that wheel."

"All finished now."

"Oh, pity. What's the news on the General?"

They squatted on the soft grass in the truck's shade, and Rick pulled out his map and said, indicating: "Here, along the Lungwebungu River, between the fourth and fifth cataracts. He's not trying to hide himself; why should he? Come to that, he couldn't even if he wanted to. A boatload of arms and ammunition arrived for him during the night. By all reports, not yet checked out, two thousand three hundred rifles and just over a quarter million rounds of ammo. He's marching east now, about fifty miles north of us."

"East?" Cass stated. "He's making it easy for us; he's heading straight for Mount Ngaru."

"No, not really. He's passed out the word that he's headed that way, and he's on more or less the right course. But my estimate is that he'll swing south during the next couple of days—Ngaru's a deathtrap for him. He'll have to take the south side of the forest."

"And Dogger's heading north. They'll pass each other by, won't they? A hundred miles apart."

"Not if I can help it, they won't."

He turned to Hamash: "Feel like a drop of the staff Irish?" He pulled out a cheap tin hip flask, sighed, and said: "Had to leave the silver one behind; it wouldn't do if someone found a beat-up old trader with a beautiful sterling silver flask in his pocket, would it?" He looked at Cass and grinned. "I've got a bottle of cognac too, out of deference to your well-developed chauvinistic hang-ups. You see how I think of the boys all the time? And if you need water, I've got a forty-gallon drum aboard, warm as a hot bath, and almost clean."

Cass tapped his canteens. "Nobody dies of thirst or hunger here—just the heat and the crying need for good cognac. You're a good man, Captain, not many of us left these days."

Rick Meyers reached under the seat and tossed the bottle to the Frenchman.

62

There was a golden rule in the Private Army, passed down and insisted upon by the Colonel himself, a drinking man if ever there was one: You can drink what you want, and as much as you want. Only God help, because I won't, the man I ever find drunk. Ever.

Cass took a long, slow swig, smacked his lips, looked at the label appreciatively, and said: "Dogger's still on the same course, headed presumably for the diamond fields, did you know that?"

"Yes, I know. He hit a Kamapa police post last night, cut off sixteen heads and displayed them on the walls around the building, a warning to anyone who might be around. The village ahead of him got the point; they've all fled into the jungle, leaving their food stores intact." He said somberly: "You're not both going in together, are you?"

Cass shook his head: "No. Paul told us your idea. And it's correct, *absolument correct.* Only I have no intention at all of letting a goddamn Turk do the work a Frenchman failed to do."

At the first strategy meeting in London, the Colonel presiding, Rick had said: "I suggest we send Cass in alone. If he gets killed, we should follow up with Hamash or one of the others, preferably Collas or Sergeant Roberts. But my first choice would be Cass Fragonard and Hamash." And so it had stood.

Hamash said, laughing softly: "I keep my distance and follow them wherever they go, a quiet and pleasant stroll through the bush while they're tearing Cass's testicles out, if he still has any, which I doubt."

Cass said: "Don't ever turn your back on me, Turk, or you'll find out, the hard way." He began to laugh, and then the buzzer in the truck's cab sounded. Rick leaned in and turned the switch, and Rudi Vicek's voice said:

"Urgent message for you from Orange, stand by, Pear Tree."

Rick said quickly: "Confidential?"

"No sir. If Apricot and Medlar are with you, it's for them too. Hold on."

In a moment Paul's voice, low and urgent, took the

place of Rudi's crisp, efficient dispassion. "Pear Tree? We've just had word—are you ready for this?—from Crocodile. It seems Fox was there at seven this morning, same deal as points three, four, and six, and the head cut off as well. Transmission interrupted in the middle of the message, but we got the idea that she may be all right and going along, do you understand what I mean?"

"I understand."

"Would that make sense to you?"

"Yes it would, under certain circumstances. She couldn't be sure, of course."

"If it's true, your friends must know. Tell them to keep their eyes and ears open. I want to reestablish, and that's important."

"Will do. They're leaving now, anything else for them?"

"Yes, a change of course. Swing west by two degrees. And Fox is a lot closer than they think. Give me Medlar, will you?"

Rick stood aside, and Cass said: "Medlar here, go ahead."

"Medlar? You'll be briefed. Crocodile is your first concern, above everything else, understand that? Crocodile first."

"*Je comprends.*"

"All right. Pear Tree? We need you here as fast as you can make it."

"Twenty-four hours, Orange."

"Good. See you then. Out."

Rick looked at Cass. He said: "Well, there's not much time, so I'll make it short. Crocodile is a woman named Leila Tunisia—she's working for us. It seems that Dogger has attacked the trading post where she's been visiting and wiped it off the face of the map, just as he did with Serimoji, Klumanana, and Omesi. At these three points everyone was murdered, but Paul seems to think Crocodile may be going along—in other words, she might have joined forces with Dogger for one ostensible reason or another . . . I don't know. She's not the type to scare easily, and she may think she can do a better job for us by getting raped every day than she can by just having her throat cut. . . . Anyway, if she's with Dogger, she's your first concern." He hesitated. "I don't like it, Cass. I don't like it at all. How often will you be able to get in touch with us?"

"If he accepts me?" He shrugged. "I'm going to try for once every night. Rudi's keeping the transmission open. I'll have three of the Mark Sevens, and Hamash is going to move them in accordance with a prearranged code. It's the best we can do."

"It should work, if you can find them. You'll be looking for a bamboo shoot among a hundred thousand bamboo shoots."

"We've got it all worked out. I'll find them."

Rick said again: "I don't like it. They'll give you a terrible time, Cass, if they even suspect you."

Cass said drily: "Just as long as they don't try and break both my legs."

"All right, you'd better be on your way. He's closer than we thought."

"Just give me the co-ordinates of Crocodile's trading post."

"Ah yes, of course."

Rick pointed to the map. "The bend of the river, here, a small village called Mkushtu. There's a steamer that makes its way north once a week, eventually reaches the Zambezi with animal hides, millet, flax, and, as often as not, a load of smuggled diamonds. There's a ship chandler, a dry-goods store, a blacksmith, a vegetable market, a butcher, and a beat-up old cafe-restaurant run by an equally beat-up Englishman named Jonas. The trading post itself, an outlet for the Algerian Export-Enterprise Company, is run by a man named Yusuf Aswani, but Paul said the head had been cut off and that presumably means he's been killed."

"They're legitimate?"

Rick shrugged. "Illegal arms, some diamond smuggling, but otherwise legitimate, yes."

Cass was peering at the map, refusing to be rushed. He said: "How wide is the river?"

"Not wide. But deep."

"How long to get his army across?"

"We don't know that. He can ford it further upstream, or he can use the existing pontoons, reinforced with logs if they're not strong enough."

"I was thinking of these heavy guns."

Rick said: "Nothing's stopped him yet, he's crossed a dozen rivers, and look at the speed he's making."

"And the Englishman is named Jonas? Jonas what?"

"Just Jonas."

"Straight?"

"A derelict. Mostly on the level, but in need, constantly, of two things."

"Money, and what else?"

"Something to bolster his lost dignity. The life of a derelict's a very hard one, and that's the heaviest cross he has to bear, the loss of his dignity. But don't trust him, Cass."

"All right." Cass straightened up. *"Merci pour le cognac."*

Rick watched them go, the loads high on their backs. He clambered aboard his truck, and set out for the long, hard drive to Mount Ngaru.

At the top of the hill, where the clear water and the orange lilies were, Cass and Hamash turned to look back. The truck was a speck in the distance now, moving fast, crashing through the light shrubbery and winding its way along the edge of the mangrove trees that reached out with their long roots for the muddy waters of the swamp. A herd of zebra was scattering before it.

Hamash looked at the sun. He said: "Two points west, Frenchman."

They walked fast among the broken yellow boulders, over the wet green moss, through the banana stands at the bank of the river—milky-grey here with poisonous minerals—and on towards the little valley where Mkushtu lay.

Mkushtu, and the Algerian Export-Enterprise Company, just recently burned to the ground and its head cut off.

CHAPTER SEVEN

MKUSHTU VILLAGE
CO-ORDINATES: 24.18E
14.01S

The people, a few of them, were straggling back into the village, looking furtively around them, the men ashamed of their fears and the women not trying to hide them.

One woman, in tears, was crouched over the embers of her house, searching through the still-hot ashes, and a child at her side was screaming. The village was an oasis on the burning plain, the empty sand around it for miles, with only the river and the trees to give it life under the hot sky: and now, death had come to the village too.

The building of the trading company, built of timber and adobe, lay half over the water's edge on the still-smouldering logs of the wharf, a ruin of charred beams that jutted out, like accusing fingers, at the sky. The mud houses around it were burned down too, and a dead cow lay in the solitary, dusty street, the carrion crows and the hawks already at work on it; by night, the hyenas would be there too. There were three other carcasses further along the road, all of them men, and an old man was dragging them to the water and throwing them in to be carried away downstream, down to where the forest was, and on and on, eventually to the Zambezi, if the predatory crocodiles hadn't taken them first. They liked dead meat, the crocodiles; they would carry the bodies under the water, deep down, and stuff them into hollows there to rot away before they were eaten.

Some trees were leaning drunkenly over the water, and further along the bank the restaurant also stood on its own wharf, and an incongruous sign, painted in black on a sheet of galvanized iron, said: *"The George and Dragon, P. Jonas, Prop."*

It was still standing. There was a palm-frond roof over a semi-verandah, a large room of whitewashed adobe, and a small building beside it which was the kitchen. A narrow corridor, only part enclosed, ran down one wall, and a man was standing there, watching, a faint air of suspicion on his face, as Cass came in.

He was a caricature of a remittance man, sixty or sixty-five years old, with grey straggling hair and a bald patch at the back, and a crumpled linen suit that had once been white, with brown suede leather ankle-boots of which the toes had been cut out for comfort. He even wore a tie, in blue-and-gold diagonal stripes, and he carried a fly swatter.

Cass looked up at the sign and said pleasantly: "You must be Mr. Jonas. What happened here?"

"Yes, I'm Jonas, what can I do for you?"

The suspicion was still there, a puzzlement added to it now. Cass said again, looking around at the shattered village: "What happened?"

"You mean you don't know?"

"How should I? I just got in."

"Then you're not—"

He scratched at a stubble of beard, no more than a day old, and tucked the frayed edge of shirt sleeve out of sight. "I thought you might have been with the raiding party, though . . . I haven't seen you before, have I? I'm afraid my memory is not . . . not what it once was. No, of course, you wouldn't be, would you—they crossed the river."

Cass was waiting.

The old man was nervous, apprehensive. He said: "We had a band of . . . of cutthroats here a little while ago, mercenaries, you understand. You must have heard of the mercenaries? They raided the trading post, killed a few people too, I'm afraid—an unpleasant lot of scoundrels." He was screwing up his eyes against the sun, squinting at Cass. "And where did you spring from? We don't have many visitors here, except when the boat comes in Mr. . . . ?"

Cass said: "Fragonard. Cass Fragonard," and held out his hand.

Jonas was delighted. He said, in execreble French: *"Fragonard? Alors, vous êtes Français, n'est-ce-pas?"*

Cass stared at him. He said pleasantly: "Well, if that's the best French you can muster, we'd better speak English, hadn't we?"

"Er, well, all right. I'm English, of course, but in the old days, at Cambridge, I was quite a French scholar. Getting a bit rusty now, I'm afraid, lack of use, y'know. But delighted to see you, delighted. We're still functioning, if there's something you'd like? A meal? Something to drink? If I can find some of the boys—they're all coming back now, I see. We do an awfully good stew, venison, mostly. With dumplings. I taught the cook how to make them myself."

"Dumplings?"

"Yes. You know, suet. *Pâte cuite*, I think it's called in French, not too sure about that. They're really very good. But why don't you come inside, it's so much cooler."

He led the way onto the verandah, pulled out a chair and clapped his hands, and a middle-aged African woman was there, standing sad and patient and looking at him, and he said to her: "Some of the stew for our guest, and some beer." He looked at Cass eagerly. "You'd like beer, wouldn't you? It's quite excellent, comes all the way from Sondola, not much of a town, really. Have you ever been there?"

"No. I came in from the west."

"Ah yes, the diamond fields, no doubt. You must know Jefferson, an old University friend of mine. Matter of fact, we were in the Guards together, too."

"No. Not the diamond fields. Where can I find Yusuf Aswani, can you tell me that?"

"Mr. Aswani? Oh dear. I'm afraid Mr. Aswani is dead. One of the casualties of the battle. Terrible people, very . . . uncouth, I think is the right word."

"Dead? *O mon Dieu.* That raises a problem. Well, I'll solve it, I suppose. Did you, eh, have any dealings with him?"

69

"With Mr. Aswani? Er, no, not really."

Was it his imagination, or had the suspicion heightened? While he was thinking about it, the African woman came back and put a chipped china plate on the table in front of him, and two bottles of beer, and when she had gone out, Jonas looked at the closing door and said: "My wife. Not as attractive as she used to be, but. . . . Well, we all grow older, don't we? What was your business with Mr. Aswani? I mean to say . . . perhaps I can help?"

Cass said gently: "How come they left you alone? Burned everything in the village except your place?"

Jonas sat down, as though he were eager to talk to someone, to anyone. He made a little gesture and said: "Well—I've nothing here they could possibly want. What would they take from me? My life? It would serve them no purpose, no purpose at all."

"What would they take from Aswani?"

"Oh, his food supplies. They were very considerable, you know. Sacks of millet, rice, corn, split peas, beans." He hesitated. "Did you ever hear of a man named Dogger?"

"Major Dogger? Yes, I've heard of him."

"A terrible man, really quite terrible."

Cass said affably: "Well, that's a matter of opinion, isn't it?"

He tackled the plate of food, his stomach turning; the heavy dumplings stuck to the roof of his mouth, and he washed them down with warm beer and said gravely: "Your *pâtes cuites* are superb."

"Oh, really? You think so? Not too soggy?"

"Delicious."

"I'm so glad." Jonas hesitated and said, peering: "But surely, about Dogger . . . you don't really approve of him, do you?"

Cass shrugged. "I neither approve, nor disapprove. But he's keeping the blacks in their place, you've got to admit that."

"Er, yes. Yes, of course." There was a little silence, and then: "Will you be staying here long, Monsieur Fragonard? I mean to say, if you'd like a bed for a few nights, we can put you up. Couple of quite reasonable rooms in the back, plenty of fresh air, all that sort of thing."

"What about Aswani's number two man? He must have had one?"

"No, there was no one else, really. A young woman came down from his head office a little while ago, but she seems to have disappeared. Probably carried off by those ruffians, I wouldn't wonder. Not the sort of people to respect a lady's integrity, I'm afraid—though she wasn't exactly a *lady*. You can always tell, can't you? Foreigner, you know. Maltese or something, by the looks of her."

Cass let him run on for a while, and when the silence came again, he took a long drink of beer and said: "Do you ever get any diamonds passing through your hands, Mr. Jonas?"

"Diamonds? Oh dear, oh *dear*. So, that's it."

"Yes, that's it. Does it worry you?"

The Englishman was nervous now, very nervous indeed. "Worry me? No, of course not. Well, that is to say. . . . Was that your business with Aswani?"

"About ten thousand dollars worth, stashed away up river. Aswani was going to take them off my hands. For cash."

Jonas was watching him carefully. "Then you knew Mr. Aswani personally?"

"No, I never met him. He sent a man to me, fellow named Hamash. Turk, or something. Told me to come in and see him. And now he's dead, so that's that. Would you have, say, half of ten thousand dollars lying around, Mr. Jonas? It's a long trek to my next prospective customer."

"Good heavens! My dear fellow, I don't have more than a few African shillings tucked away, shillings, not even pounds, not even enough to get me out of this . . . this confounded hole." He said hastily: "Of course, when I first came here, it was quite different; I had six personal servants in those days, just had to raise my finger . . . I don't mean *staff*. I had a manager to worry about them, and I must say, he treated them awfully well, I mean servants, six of them. . . . The African woman you saw was one of them, she was the cook's helper. I had my own boat on the river, a yacht if you please, and trade was bloody marvelous—incense, hides, a little tungsten once in a while; this was a thriving business, I can tell you. And then. . . . Well, independence came, and we were all out of a job. All my British staff chose to go home, but . . . Well, it would have been hard for me to do that, for forty years I'd never felt pavement under my feet, thought I'd never adjust to it. And then things started running down, the trade stopped coming, there were no tourists, no safaris, not even the crocodile hunters any more; they were taxed out of business. Same story all over Africa, the white man goes and his place is taken by . . . by Indians, and Arabs, and . . . and God knows what, the whole place runs downhill so fast. . . ."

Cass was astonished to see that the old man was almost in tears. He said sympathetically: "Change is always for the worse, isn't it? Never for the better."

"How right, how *very* right! It was marvelous in those days, bloody marvelous, clap your hands and they came running, called you 'bwana,' or 'sahib,' or 'master'. . . . Paid them a few shillings a month, a handful of flour and some beans. . . . Mark you, they were happy. Catch them off guard and ask them, and they'll tell you, they were happier then, they considered it an honor to serve us, and by God, it was. And then . . ." he sighed, "independence, and look at me now." He brightened suddenly, an almost mischievous smile on his face, and said: "But you know? It doesn't really *matter,* Monsieur Fragonard, does it? As long as we hold on to our dignity. That's something they can never take away from us, something we're born to. They're envious of it, but they can't take it away from us."

Cass said quietly: "And Dogger's trying to arrest that progress, isn't he? You see what I mean?"

"Yes. Yes, indeed I do. Would you care for some more of our ragout? It's excellent, isn't it?"

Cass pushed his plate away, "No thank you, Mr. Jonas, not now. But if I could put my feet up on the verandah rail, and rest for a while, and have some more beer and wonder what I'm going to do next . . . ? Could I do that?"

72

"Of course, my dear fellow, make yourself comfortable."

Jonas was beaming now, a happy man again. He stood up and said: "If you'll excuse me, I have to check on the boys; they've got to be kept on their toes. I'll send someone in with some more beer."

When he had gone, Cass put his feet up on the railing, leaned back in his rickety chair, closed his eyes, and waited.

The sun was beginning to sink, four hours later, when the seeds he had planted began to sprout.

The village was filling up again now, and the noise of shouting men was still mingled with the screams and the tears of the wailing women. He heard them coming and opened his eyes, and Jonas was there, beaming, another man with him now.

He looked him over quickly, wondering if this were Dogger himself. A big bearded man in blue denims, with the sleeves of his jacket cutoff at the shoulders, a string of hand grenades round his belt and a German FG42 automatic rifle slung lightly over his shoulder, the 7.92mm. gas-operated rifle that would cycle at 600 rpm, its lightweight tripod discarded. There was a Luger 9mm. .08 stuck in the top of his trousers, and a long hunting knife in a scabbard at his left thigh. Left-handed, then . . .

Jonas said: "Monsieur Fragonard, this is Captain Karnobat."

Karnobat? One of the Bulgarians, then?

Cass held out his hand, and Karnobat took it perfunctorily and sat down and said: "Where did you come from, Fragonard?"

"On this trip, from Luso, in Angola."

"How'd you get here?"

"Down the river on the steamer, over the border to Chavuma, by truck to Kabompo, and then on foot. Took me four days."

"And you came looking for Aswani?"

"That's right."

"If you've got some stuff for him, maybe you'd like to

73

sell it to me instead? Ten thousand dollars worth, Jonas says. On the IDB market, that means about thirty-five hundred."

The IDB were the illicit diamond buyers, a force to be reckoned with in these parts, and Cass said mildly: "I was hoping for five, Captain Karnobat."

"I'd have to see them first. Where are they?"

"They're hidden in a tree outside Kabompo."

"That's forty miles from here. Are you a pro?"

"IDB? No, not really. This is a load I just . . . happened on by chance." He had the idea that Karnobat wasn't very interested in the mythical diamonds. "I should get five thousand for them, if I can get the right buyer."

"Then what's your line of work?"

Fragonard shrugged. "Oh, trader, ship navigator, hunter. . . . I was a prospector for a while in Botswana, got thrown out by the blacks, tried my hand at road-building in Zambia, but I never got paid, so I gave that up, no profit in it."

"Before that?"

"Oh, pissing around Africa—all kinds of things a man can put his hand to if he's got a head on his shoulders."

"A hunter, you said?"

"That's right. Lion, elephant, crocs . . . I'm a pretty fair shot."

"You know how to use a gun like this?" Karnobat held out the FG42, and Cass said: "Sure. But that's not a hunting rifle, it's a machine gun."

"Try it on single shot." He tossed the gun easily over, and Cass pulled over the lever to single and looked at the river below them. Karnobat picked up an empty beer bottle and tossed it high in the air, and Cass fired from the hip, aiming instinctively, and shattered it before it hit the water. He got off his second shot as the biggest chunk of it hit the mud, and blew it back into the river. He flicked open the breech and gravely handed the gun back, and Karnobat said, not changing his expression: "You didn't learn to shoot a forty-two like that hunting lions, Fragonard."

"For lions," Cass said, "I use my bare hands."

Karnobat's stolid look had still not changed. He was neither scowling nor smiling, nor showing any interest at all; a robot, Cass was thinking. He said: "All right, where did you learn to fire a forty-two?"

"The Foreign Legion. It was our standard weapon for a while."

Now there was a glimmer of interest. "How long ago was that?"

"First term in Sidi Bel Abbes, Algeria, nineteen thirty to nineteen thirty-six. Left them, went back when World War Two broke out, and was with the Fourth Camel Corps in Syria, transferred to Tanks, went back to Algeria, invalided out when I lost my legs." He tapped his thigh with his knuckles and said: "Aluminum, best kind of leg there is."

"You ever hear of Major Dogger?"

"Sure, who hasn't heard of him?"

"Do you like what he's doing?"

Cass shrugged. "*Mon Dieu,* what the hell do I care about what he's doing? As long as he leaves me alone, I'll leave him alone. It's none of my damn business."

"You have any ties? Like a wife?"

"No."

"A mistress, maybe? Anything like that?"

"At my age?"

Karnobat grunted: "Major Dogger is my boss. You want to come and work for him?"

Cass shook his head. "No. I don't know enough about him."

"Like *what* don't you know?" His voice was thickly accented, the K's deep in the throat.

"I don't know what he pays, and I don't work for nothing, not for anybody."

Karnobat was mocking now: "He was in the Foreign Legion too, an old buddy maybe, so why don't we go and ask him if he'd like to take you on? Twelve miles from here, think you can make it on those aluminum legs of yours?"

"What about my diamonds?"

"The hell with your diamonds. We don't deal in no

three thousand dollars. You want to come on your own two feet, or shall I drag you there?"

Cass said easily: "Don't try it, Captain. It never pays off." He got to his feet lightly and said: "Let's go."

Karnobat dug into his pocket and came up with a gold coin, one of the old French five franc pieces. He tossed it contemptuously at Jonas, and followed Cass down the broken steps of the verandah.

Jonas said: "Thank you, Captain, you're very kind." He raised his voice and called out after them: "Did I tell you Monsieur Fragonard, that I was in the Guards?"

The sun was going down now, and they crossed the swiftly flowing river over the old pontoon and walked through the jungle for four hours in the darkness, following a well-defined trail that had been recently blazed.

There was little of the moon's light under the trees; Karnobat used his flashlight frequently, and Fragonard said sarcastically: "If you can't see in the dark, Captain, why don't you let me lead the way?"

Karnobat said nothing, and the stolid look on his dark face did not change. The night noises of the forest were shrill and insistent.

A sentry challenged them, and then another and another and another, Africans all of them, in uniform and carrying Sten guns, and soon they came to a clearing where a crude shelter had been built of palm fronds over bent stakes, and when the Captain whistled, a man came out of it and stared at them, and said:

"What the hell are you doing here, Karnobat? You're supposed to be rear guard." He looked hard at Fragonard. "And who the hell's this? What's he doing here?"

Karnobat said: "Recruit. And the rear guard's okay, Hans is there. This fellow's name is Fragonard—at least, that's what he calls himself. He tried to sell me a couple of dollars worth of diamonds, but he's pretty fancy with a gun, and I thought another white man might be useful to us. He's out of the Legion, Major." He jerked his head and said: "This is Major Dogger, and you call him sir."

Dogger said: "The Legion? Well, that's nice. When were you there, Fragonard?"

"Sidi Bel Abbes in nineteen thirty, sir."

"Long before my time. Who was your commanding officer?"

"Colonel Trenchant, sir."

"Trenchant? Oh yes, he retired, I believe, about nineteen thirty-eight."

He was a tightly muscled man of forty-five or so, with close-cropped iron-grey hair and a deep tan, in a jungle camouflage suit and a khaki beret. His eyes were very sharp and alert, and he moved with an absolute economy of effort. He looked somehow *dangerous*.

But his manner now was courteous, even affable, and he said: "My C.O. was Fauroy, a good officer—he must have been a lieutenant in your time. We'll have a lot to talk about, won't we? Would you like to come and work for me? We've a lot of hard fighting ahead of us, no Tauregs this time, just a lot of blacks, but a very great number of them. I can use all the good men I can get."

Karnobat said laconically: "He's worried about the pay, Major."

"Oh, I see. Well, my officers, the white men, are all paid the same—one thousand American dollars a month. It's paid into a bank in Bulawayo, but you can draw on it in the field if you ever need to, which doesn't often happen. But if it does, then you have to accept East African pounds, or French francs, or whatever money we happen to have at the moment. Everything found, of course, and we're well financed; there's never any doubt about the money, as all the officers will tell you."

His hands were flat on the back of his hips, and he was stretching his shoulder muscles, flexing them as though he suffered from arthritis. He smiled genially and said: "I can't accept you, of course, without a great deal of questioning. Some of that must have been done already, or Karnobat wouldn't have brought you here, but . . . In the morning, Fragonard. I'll be busy for the rest of the night, but come to my tent at five o'clock, and we'll talk. Karnobat will find you somewhere to sleep until then."

He nodded, and went back into the tent.

As the woven flap was pulled aside, Cass saw there, by

the flare of a kerosene lamp, a woman stretched out on a camp cot. She was naked, and there was the curve of the breast and a long, smooth hip gleaming in the yellow light, and then the flap fell into place again, and Karnobat was saying: "This way, friend."

They pushed their way through the tightly confining trees to a second small clearing where a fire was burning, around which a dozen or so men were sitting, the flames lighting their tough and battle-scarred faces. There was the ripe smell in the air of roasting venison, and at another fire, close by, an African was turning a carcass on a crude spit. The men were passing round a bottle of *tendiri*, the harsh liquor made from palm leaves infused with ginger, and they looked up as the two new arrivals came into the firelight.

Karnobat said, indicating the men perfunctorily: "This is Fragonard, gentlemen, a real tough ex-Legionnaire." He was using his thumb, indicating the others carelessly: "Hendrix, Russo, Flammer, Christenson, Manera, Voskovic, Ball, Zukor, Perrot, Balcovici, the two Ujpest brothers, and Lederer. And, there's a matter we have to attend to right away, isn't there?"

He turned to Cass and looked at him coldly, and then tossed his rifle to one of the men, took out his luger and tossed that to another, and said: "Now, I said I might have to drag you here, and what was it you said, Fragonard?"

Cass said mildly: "I suggested it wouldn't be wise to try it, Captain."

They were standing close together, very close, and Karnobat brought up a sudden knee, very hard, into Cass's groin, and Cass stepped back and twisted sideways, and struck at it with an aluminum leg, a hard, sharp, and deadly blow, and the Captain went sprawling in the wet earth, lying there and looking up in shocked surprise.

The long hunting knife was already in his hand when he leaped up, grimacing at the pain of a cracked kneecap, and he stood in a crouch and waited, and Cass smiled and said: "Are you coming at me, or shall I come at you? It's all the same, Captain."

The men around the fire had gotten to their feet and were forming a circle round them, and one of them said, jeering: "You don't need the knife, Karnobat, he's old enough to be your grandfather."

He did not take his eyes off Cass. He said slowly: "Oh, I'm not going to hurt him, the Major wants to see him in the morning. I'm just going to cut his ears off, make him hear good. . . ."

He waited, and Cass advanced a trifle, and the Captain feinted with the knife to his belly and then swung it high in a savage and lightning-quick arc, up and over and across. He was astonished that the Frenchman's head seemed just not to be there any more; he did not see the quick sideways bend as the foot came up again, kicking hard and fast and aimed with deadly accuracy at the side of his neck. He took the blow under the ear and swung round away from it, and the other foot came up, hard metal, and caught him once in the throat and once more under the ear. He went down and vomited, and as he lay there on the ground, the Frenchman leaned over and picked him up like a baby, all hundred and ninety-five pounds and six feet of him, with one firm hand tangled in his hair, and the other cupped under his chin.

He held him there for a moment, staggering, and as he let him fall he stepped back quickly and shot out a foot, the instep twisted away, and hit him hard in the middle of the chest, a stunning blow on the solar plexus.

Karnobat went down and lay still, and one of the men came over, grinning, and held out a hand.

Cass said warily: "No. I might need my hands too."

The other man threw back his head and laughed. "Perrot, Gaston Perrot, from Marseilles. And I haven't seen *savate* like that since I left home. *Bienvenu, mon vieux,* you are welcome here."

They were gathered around him now, laughing and jostling him, a dull evening livened up. One of them— was it the man named Balcovici?—said: "Watch out for Karnobat when he comes round. He will kill you."

"No," Cass said. "Didn't you hear? The Major wants to see me in the morning."

Some of them were looking him over sullenly, not liking the turn of events at all, but the two who had been called the Ujpest brothers, young and blond and boyish, were clapping him on the back and laughing, and one of them passed him the *tendiri* bottle, and he took a long, grateful swig of it, and grimaced; he wished he had kept the bottle of good cognac that Rick Meyers had offered him.

He joined the others at the fire, and sat and chatted with them for a while, and when he at last pulled a blanket over his head to keep the nighttime dew out, Karnobat was still unconscious, left alone and neglected there on the humid forest floor.

He listened to the sounds of the others snoring, and lay awake all night and waited.

And he was thinking: Well, now I'm where I'm supposed to be. And how, *pour l'amour de Dieu,* am I ever going to make contact with Hamash?

CHAPTER EIGHT

MOUNT NGARU
CO-ORDINATES: 22.40E
              12.05S

You could stand on the top of the mountain and look around you carefully with binoculars, and you would never have seen that any changes whatsoever had been made in its jagged, broken contours.

On what had become known as Level Three, a little more than a hundred feet from the topmost peak, the trailing vines had altered their course and were now running, not among the bamboo plants, but a little to one side of them, climbing over a woven laticework of mangrove poles that had been brought up from the edge of the swamp and that covered a sunken shelter, sixteen feet by twenty-four feet and six feet deep, where the advance party of the Private Army had set up its sophisticated electronic equipment.

Paul had said: "If a man walks by here, tracking down game, hunting for wild mushrooms, or looking for clear water, I want him to see nothing amiss, *nothing*. More than that, if he's been sent here to search us out, I want him to go back and say to Dogger or Lincoln or whomever it may be: 'There's nothing there at all, *nothing* . . .' I want to see no freshly dug earth, no trailing wires, no footprints. And I want to hear no sounds. From now on, we keep our voices down, down, *down*."

The vines had covered the headquarters completely, the dark green of them interspersed with the bright pink of hypericum bushes and the brilliant flames of the red-hot poker. A small trench had even been scooped out around them and kept dampened with water, so that the colors would not fade and give the impression that the plants had been interfered with.

Below this HQ, on the southern side, the gentle slope overlooked the plain where the round boulders were, and here, every hundred feet, a large foxhole had been dug (the sand carefully scattered to blend with the rest of the topsoil) and covered over with grass and twigs and clumps of living castor.

Paul Tobin and Major Bramble were in the main shelter, where Rudi Vicek sat at the console of his main receiver, and the large-scale maps were spread out on the canvas roll-up table in front of them. The maps were all covered with the small, precise lettering of Betty de Haas, to which Drima had added some comments of his own, now that he himself had seen the land and inspected it.

On the scope at the console, the needle was flickering through the tiny pinpoint of light, bleeping its way round quietly, and Vicek, said: "Moretti, sir. He's seven miles off at four thousand feet."

Paul got to his feet and looked at the scope. "Seven miles? All right, open communications." He poured himself half a tumbler of Irish whisky and sipped it, and heard Vicek say: "Ready when you are, Skylark."

The static was crackling as Moretti's boyish voice came in: "Stand by for message, Orange, and I've got a drop for you too."

Vicek said sharply: "Trim your set, Skylark! Drop on the finder, I'll open up for you, frequency seven thirty-two." He spun the dial and said: "Seven thirty-two open, go ahead."

Moretti said: "They've left the river, and it looks like they moved through the forest during the day, though I couldn't spot them, too much cover. Cooking fires along the route though, and I've pinpointed them for you. They came to the swamp at sixteen hundred hours and moved along the edge of it, eighty-seven degrees. When the light went, they'd covered roughly twelve miles, so if they're still moving they should be at point forty-two. Hold on, I'm coming over the finder."

The speaker went dead, and Vicek looked at the tiny orange light, flickering now as the plane approached its target. It changed abruptly to green, and Vicek zoomed in the dish of the scope and watched the pinprick of white light, tilting the dish slowly down to keep the contact centered, and said softly: "He's made the drop, package released and coming down, he's four hundred feet off, he must have wind up there."

The green light went out and the speaker came on again, and Moretti said: "I'm picking up a signal from two hundred and thirty meters to the west of the finder—have you got trouble down there? I can't identify it. . . ."

Paul picked up the speaker. "It's all right, Skylark, we know about that."

Ever since darkness had come, Aklilu, Collas, and Sergeant Roberts had been stringing out the long line of sensors, planting them at tactical intervals in the ground; some of them—the Mark Sevens—were alive, and gave out a constant signal of their own, activated or not, that could be picked up on the plane's hypersensitive radio.

Paul said: "What's in the drop, Skylark?"

"Maps, mostly, Orange. Some personal stuff from home, for you and for Orange two. Do you want me to go south?"

"No, south is taken care of, stick with the same route."

He nodded and put down the mike, and Vicek said: "What's the wind speed up there?"

They could hear Moretti's quiet laugh. He said: "What the hell do you care what the wind speed is up here? It's forty-seven point four—are you worried I'll miss the bloody target?"

Drima's voice broke in from down below there under he umbrella thorns: "Drop recovered, Orange. It's on target." Vicek grinned and said: "You're all right, Skylark, anything else?"

"Yes. I want to go to the bathroom."

"Over and out."

He switched off and went back to testing the sensors, checking them off on the chart as Sergeant Robert's voice came in from time to time: "Eight-three in position. . . . Eighty-four in position. . . . Eighty-five in seventy feet on ninety-two, hard rocks there. . . . Eighty-six in position. . . . I'm skipping eighty-seven and eighty-eight,

eighty-nine on a rise will do the job of both of them. . . .
Ninety in position. . . ."

Paul said: "Nothing from Cass Fragonard yet."

"Nothing, sir."

He sat down and glared at the map, and Bramble said:
"Don't worry, it's still early."

"Yes. Yes, I suppose it is." He thumped at the chart
with his fist and said: "Why hasn't Lincoln turned south
yet? Can you tell me that? He's coming straight this way,
and I don't believe it. If he tries to climb this mountain,
we're going to be in hell's own trouble. I've half a mind to
order in the glider right now."

The chart was pinpointed with Lincoln's movements—
as far as they were known—and two carefully drawn lines,
one in red and one in blue, traced alternate courses among
the natural obstructions that he might meet. The red code
was marked: *Probable route,* and the blue one: *First alternative.*

It was a sand-table operation, Paul was thinking, with
the opposing armies moved by academy students carrying
long mahogany batons in accordance with an ancient pattern; only here, the pattern had not yet taken place.

Bramble was calm, sure that in this juggling of the two
involuntary forces the only answer was to estimate their
strategy, and to stay with the answer till it was proven con-
clusively wrong.

He said, frowning: "Either he doesn't know where Dogger is, which I don't believe, or he's hoping that Dogger is
watching every move he makes and will deduce he's going
to the north of the quicksand. In which case, Dogger will
slip in behind him, and that'll put him exactly where, I
imagine, Lincoln would like him to be—on the southern
bank of the Mwombejhi River."

Paul pulled out the large-scale map and studied it intently. He said, musing: "The Mwombejhi . . . Yes, I
like that. There's only one thing wrong with it."

"Oh? What's that?"

"Dogger will never fall for it. The Mwombejhi would
give Lincoln too much advantage. If Dogger ran into trouble he couldn't retreat. If he wanted to bring his reserves

in, he'd have to bring them in from the left, where they're terribly vulnerable, because he couldn't move his guns across the swamp on his right. I don't think he'll accept those conditions."

Bramble was shaking his head. He said stubbornly: "We have to remember the man's psychology. Everything we know about Dogger indicates that he only uses his wits when he's up against a well-organized force that can be expected to have at least a competent idea of what the word *tactics* mean. In other words—mercenaries. It's axiomatic in these African battles that whichever side has the mercenaries wins. Because they're the professionals, the experts, and so far Dogger's only been up against untrained—or insufficiently trained—Africans, except on one or two rare occasions, and those are the occasions we have to study now. In Biafra, you remember, he charged through everything, a bull in a china shop, till the Nigerians threw Rolf Steiner and his mercenaries against him. Then, and not till then, he started using his wits, he started *thinking* instead of just lashing out ferociously. This time he's up against a black army, no white mercenaries to lead them. We have to consider what he'll make of that."

"You mean his contempt for them?"

"I mean *exactly* that."

Paul added: "You may be right. He outnumbers them a trifle, he's got heavy guns which they haven't, and yes, he has a weakness. His overconfidence just might put him on the bank of the Mwombejhi. And that just might be Guevara Lincoln's thinking too. He got his training in China and Algeria—and in both those places they're pretty strong on the psychological aspect of the enemy's strategy." He went back to the small-scale map and said: "Leila Tunisia suggested that there were less than a thousand men in the attack on the trading post. I wonder where his main body is?"

"That's what I'm hoping Cass will tell us."

"Yes. Cass. We've got to get their main body where we want it, and we don't even know where it's at. I'm beginning to think our plan's too rigid."

It was one of the Colonel's favorite maxims: *No plan survives contact with the enemy. . . .*

Bramble said firmly: "No. I still say he'll swing south during the night."

"Two enemies," Paul said and sighed. "It's always twice as hard."

The first concept that the Colonel had drilled into them was: *Get inside your enemy's mind . . . Find out first what he's likely to do, given the kind of man he is.*

And with two of them, the chess game became three-dimensional. If A does this, then B must do that, and therefore C—that's me—must do . . .

But if B doesn't react the way we think he should, or if A makes the wrong first step, then C is out on a limb and the mission's a failure.

And that was the one thing, failure, that the Colonel would never stand for.

Paul said out loud, apropos his own thoughts: "My God, I believe the shock would kill him. . . ."

Bramble stared at him and said nothing.

The expected message from Cass did not come till seven forty-eight in the morning. They had been up all through the night, waiting for it.

Rudi Vicek threw the switch when the three red lights began to flicker in unison, and said quickly: "Here he is now, sir." He corrected himself and said calmly: "Medlar coming in."

Paul said urgently: "Switch to speaker, make no acknowledgement."

"No acknowledgement, sir."

"Not till we know he can receive safely."

"All ready, sir."

They waited.

Bramble had risen and was sitting on the edge of the rock slab that was the table for the oversize maps, lighting his pipe—a small pack of his favorite tobacco that Betty, bless her heart, had included in his personal drop during the night—and listening to the thumping of his heart. He was thinking: If he's got anything for us, anything at all, it's the beginning we've all been waiting for.

They heard Cass's voice, loud and clear and seeming very close indeed: *"Ici nefle, mes amis . . ."* and Bram said, puzzled: *"Nefle?* What the hell's he talking about?"

Paul said, grinning: "Medlar is French, he's in good spirits."

Cass said again: *"C'est à dire,* Medlar. Come in if you can hear me, I do not like talking to a bamboo shoot; it makes me look idiotic. Come in, please."

Rudi was looking at Paul, but Paul shook his head and waited, and the voice said again: "Come in, Orange."

A silence, and then: "Ah yes, *je comprends.* Yes, you can talk, provided you don't shout too much. My personal bodyguard is five hundred meters behind me, hiding in a tree and thinking I don't know he's there, so you may talk. Come in, please."

Paul nodded, and Rudi pushed over the lever, and Paul said: "Cass, you don't know how relieved we all are. What's that about a personal bodyguard?"

"All right, if we're in clear . . . Paul, I have joined forces with our friend; he's paying me one thousand American dollars a month, a bank in Rhodesia. He doesn't trust me yet, though there's no reason why he shouldn't, and he's having me watched. Or maybe his second in command is, that's Captain Karnobat, one of the Bulgarians. I've been sent out on the left flank, alone, but a man named Christenson has been following me very carefully all morning."

Paul said: "Co-ordinates, Cass, you're forgetting."

"I didn't want to carry a map, it would have looked suspicious, but I'm about eight miles due northwest of Mkushtu village, which has been completely destroyed. I'm sitting in the grass talking to a bamboo shoot, *très ridicule,* your voice coming to me from it very nicely, also *très ridicule.* There are roughly one thousand men in the column; I don't know, not yet, where the main force is, or if it even exists. I think it does, because there are only fifteen officers here, and we know that he has more than that. He has a Marseilles Frenchman with him; I hope to have a chat with him when we get together again."

"And Crocodile?"

Cass said: "I think she is here. I cannot be sure. If she is—she is safe."

"Are you sure of that?"

Cass hesitated. He said at last: "Paul, I saw a woman in his bed, but who she was I don't know. I'm guessing. I'll know more later."

"All right. What about Hamash?"

"He was here, Paul, I saw him; he's keeping well under cover. He moved off when he saw I'd read the code properly and knew where to look for the transmitter, so presumably he had spotted Christenson back there, watching me. I'm assuming he's nearby somewhere, but he's well out of sight at the moment. I may, or may not, get a chance to talk with him. He still has three more Mark Sevens, so he's almost certainly listening in on us."

They all heard Hamash's guarded voice breaking in on them: "Yes, I'm here, eight hundred meters on forty-three from Cass. If you have anything for me . . . ?"

Paul said: "No. Just keep up the good work. Cass? Are you moving on now?"

"Yes, I must, very soon."

"Pull up the sensor and bury it."

"Of course, you think I am just a beginner?"

"Do you know where you're heading?"

"We rendezvous at Busanga Hook, the south-edge corner of the Busanga Flats, one hour after sundown . . . Wait." In a moment, he said quickly: "Christenson coming in. I'm signing off."

He dropped to his knees and started digging in the soft sand with both hands, like an animal, and then he slipped off his trousers and crouched over the hole. When Christenson came up he was squatting there and scratching at his belly, and he looked up, surprised, and said: "Christenson! I thought you were with the main party."

He was Swedish, a wiry, sunburned man with almost white hair and a sharp, pointed beard, and he carried a Schmeisser machine-pistol, its safety catch always off.

He said: "What the hell are you up to, Fragonard?"

Cass shrugged. "I would have thought you could see that." He wiped his behind carefully with a stone, dropped it into the hole, and kicked sand in, kicking in the bamboo shoot too, and did up his trousers and said again: "You can see what I'm doing. Who told you to follow me?"

"That's none of your business, and you're wasting time."

"Dropping a load of crap is never a waste of time. Constipation is bad for the soul."

"And you're more than a kilometer off course. Busanga's over there." He pointed.

"I know that," Cass said. "If you think the shortest route through the bush is always the quickest, you're an idiot."

He hoisted the rifle they had given him over his shoulder and walked away, not once looking back.

Paul said: "Busanga. That's very interesting, isn't it?"

The large-scale map was in place again, and Bramble was reading aloud from Betty's annotation: " . . . and a bend of deep water, known locally as Busanga Hook, is in the center of the swamp's edge at its narrowest point. On each side, the most treacherous reaches of the swamp curve round in a crescent pointing south, the two arms coming to within eight or nine hundred yards of each other. The entire Kowala tribe was massacred here by the Odishis during one of the tribal wars that took place immediately after Independence, when they found there was no way out of the trap they had been led into. Each arm of the crescent is about thirty miles long . . ."

He looked up and said: "That means that as soon as they rendezvous, he's got to backtrack for thirty miles or more. It doesn't make sense, does it?"

"No, it doesn't," Paul said. "Except that the Hook's at the narrowest point—I think that's vital."

"You mean he's going to try and cross it? With heavy guns?"

"We don't know where the guns are, do we? They might be there already."

"For what conceivable purpose . . ." Bramble began. He broke off and peered at the map and said: "Ah yes, a good stand of trees within half a mile of him. It's possible."

"More than possible. Cass says he's got only a thousand men, and fifteen officers. The rest are with the guns, but why does he need such a large force of Africans on what is patently the second unit? After all, Dogger himself is with the smaller force, which we must therefore call his main body. . . . Seven or eight thousand men, with a large stand of trees close by. . . . They could build pontoons, or a bridge, clear across that swamp in the course of a single night. Its narrowest point, less than three miles across. A bridge, a few inches below the surface of the water; black water, you could pass within inches of it and not see a damn thing."

"Tenuous," Bramble said.

"Give me a better reason to put him in the middle of a thirty-mile dead end."

Bramble thought about it for a while. He said at last: "Yes, I think you're right. He's going to cross it. One way or another." He began to draw a third projected route for Major Dogger, a neat yellow line across the map, and said: "That would bring him right into Lincoln's present projection, unless, as we think he has, Lincoln turned south during the night. But if we're *wrong* about Lincoln, and *right* about Dogger then they'll meet head-on within forty-eight hours, and in the worst possible place for us."

Paul said: "We'll assume our deductions are correct, at least till we hear either from Moretti again, or from Edgars, who ought to be in position pretty soon now. What's Aklilu doing?"

"Setting out sensors."

"I want him to go down and take a look at Busanga Hook."

"But . . ." Bramble frowned. "We'll know the next time Cass comes on the air, Paul. . . ."

"In case he doesn't, Bram."

"All right." He turned to Rudi. "How many sensors out, Rudi?"

Vicek flicked the pages of his chart. "They're up to three hundred and eighty-two; they'll have the rest out by about three o'clock tomorrow morning."

"So get Aklilu in."

"Yes sir."

A cool breeze was drifting through the shelter. Closed on three sides by sandstone, the room was ventilated with tunnels that had been hollowed out on the eastern side, where the wind came from. On its south, which was open, it looked down under the overhang or camouflage plantings onto the boulder valley below.

Aklilu came in, sweating, and Paul showed him the map and pointed out Busanga Hook, and said: "How long will it take you to get down there, take a quick look at the swamp, see if there's a bridge under the mud across it, and get back up here?"

Aklilu said: "In a hurry, Major?"

"In a hurry."

He studied the map for a moment. "An over-all incline of one in three, a detour around the cliff on the way back . . . Say, twenty-four hours?"

"It's sixty miles, Aklilu. And tough going all the way."

"Maybe only twenty hours. I can be there in seven and a half, it's the climb back that will take the time." He shrugged. "Call it twenty, and I'll try for eighteen."

Paul looked at his watch and smiled. "It's now eight fifty-five. This time tomorrow morning. All I want to know is, have they put a bridge across from Busanga Hook, south to north? If they have, it'll be a few inches under the surface, and it won't be easily visible except from close up."

"The guns, if they're there, are on the south?"

"Yes."

"Then I can inspect it on the northern side, it's going to be . . ." He saw the look on Paul's face, and said: "All right, Major. You want to know about the guns too. So, this time tomorrow morning at the latest."

"Get going, Aklilu."

The Ethiopian nodded. He ducked outside, and in a few moments Paul took the binoculars and went outside too,

91

and stood among the lilies looking down the steep slope of the hill.

Aklilu had shucked off his uniform jumpsuit, and was dressed in a loincloth and carrying a spear and a bow with a small quiver of arrows over his left shoulder, a local tribesman, and he was running fast down to the valley, a steady, even trot, his legs pumping, his bare feet pounding the broken, rocky surface.

Paul watched him for a long time, admiring the steady rhythm of his running. He flicked the switch of the range finder, looked at his watch, and saw that in exactly five minutes the Ethiopian had covered a trifle over a mile.

CHAPTER NINE

KONDARUGU
CO-ORDINATES: 23.18E
               13.18S

Edgars Jefferson had spent a full hour with the long, supple locust branch, flipping it over his shoulder, alone out there in the bush (with no one to see the tears he could hardly hold back), and dragging the great recurved thorns of it across his back.

Some of the self-inflicted gashes were a quarter of an inch deep, and when he thought he might be losing too much blood, he put a stop to it thankfully and lay down in the cold wood ashes of the fire he had made for the purpose, rolling around and squirming till he had covered his back with a paste of ash and blood and had stopped the bleeding, or most of it.

Was it only a day ago? The pain was still insufferable, and he knew what it was they were doing; someone was rubbing dry rock salt into the wounds, opening them up again and causing the brittle, searing pains to shoot through to the back of his head.

He lay on his naked belly, his arms and legs stretched out and staked down into the mud, and the mud was finding its way into his mouth and stifling him, and still they kept on rubbing in the raw salt, and he screamed. He heard the General say: "You know, Abdul Karan, I'm beginning to believe this boy."

He twisted his head round and saw the tall and dignified figure, the uniform spotless and well pressed, standing beside him and staring somberly down at him.

He said, whining: "Please sir, master, don't beat me no more."

The General said, frowning: "Where did you learn to speak English like that, boy?"

93

He spat some mud out of his mouth and said: "At home, sir, master, in Monrovia."

He saw the General look at the other man—was he a Sudanese?—and the other man nodded and said: "Yes, it could be."

"You ever been to Chicago, boy? You ever been to the States?"

"No sir, master, I never been there. Liberia, Nigeria, Congo, Rhodesia . . ."

"We don't call it Rhodesia, boy. We call it Zambia, or Botswana."

"Yes sir, master, Zambia."

"And what were you doing in Zambia?"

"My master took me there, sir. Please, sir, let me go? I'm . . . I'm scared."

"I'll bet you are, boy. You got plenty to be scared about. Who beat you across the back like that?"

"My master, sir."

"That why you ran away?"

"Yes sir. He was like to kill me next time, sir."

"White man?"

"Yes sir."

"Servant?"

"Yes sir. Houseboy."

"You just black trash, boy." The General spat at him and said angrily: "Ain't you got no dignity? How come you want to be houseboy to that white man? How come you didn't up and kill him when he beat you like that?"

There was a long, long silence, and he was thinking: Christ, he's not going to believe a word of it. The story he had rehearsed seemed full of flaws to him now. Was the pain affecting his judgement?

The General said at last, very gently: "You tried to kill that white man?"

"No sir, not really, only . . ." He broke off, coughing blood.

"Only what, boy?"

"Only . . . the white man's cook, he said to him, you watch out, master, for that Edgars, he sure gonna make trouble for you one day, he like to kill you maybe. And so the white man he take me and say, Edgars, I'm going to beat you within an inch of your life, teach you who's boss around here. And that's what he done, master, he beat me bad till the blood come, and I upped and ran away, and if I ever see him again I'm sure going to kill him, yes sir master."

"Edgars? Is that your name?"

"Yes sir, master. Edgars Jefferson."

"Jefferson? That's a right proud name you got." He turned to the Sudanese. "What am I going to do with this black man, Abdul Karan?"

Abdul Karan shrugged. "I never have to tell you what to do, Guevara. Seems to me he feels badly enough about a critical subject to be useful to us." He looked at Edgars. "Do you know how to use a gun?"

"Yes sir. My master used to make me load for him, carry his rifles. I don't shoot too good, I don't think, but yes sir, I know how to use one."

"Cut him loose," the General said.

One of the soldiers who was there drew his knife across the thongs, and Edgars staggered to his feet and rubbed at the blood on his wrists. He said: "Can I . . . can I have my clothes back, master, sir?"

"You get a uniform, boy, you're going to hold your head high."

He gestured, and a young girl came running with a pair of khaki trousers. The General took them from her and tossed them over, and said: "You wear these now; they give you sandals, a jacket. They find out if you really can use a gun."

He said to Abdul Karan: "We don't have any Liberians, do we? Better put him with Captain Entoro, give him some training."

He turned back to Edgars. "We're going to put a gun in your hands, Edgars. You better learn to use it, else you ain't no good to me at all. And then we're going to fight, to fight a white devil named . . ." He broke off. "You ever go to school, Edgars?"

"Yes sir. Monrovia. High School."

"Then I don't have to talk to you about white devils,

and bullets turning to water, do I? You're an educated man, and maybe an educated African or two is what I need. All right, we're going to fight a man named Dogger; he leads a pigsty full of mercenaries, white men, and he's got. . . ."

In the silence, he was staring at the look on Edgars' face. He said at last, thoughtfully: "Did I say something, boy? I say something that startled you?"

"N-n-no, sir."

"Dogger. Looked to me like when I said that name you was like to die. Major Dogger. You ever hear tell of him?"

Edgars was whimpering now, and he was thinking: Christ, no wonder they threw you out of the Panthers, you don't have the brains of a goat. But he nodded his head, shakily, and said: "Yes, sir. I heard tell of him."

"And he scares you, is that it? You don't have to be scared!" He said angrily: "We've got eight, nine, ten thousand black men going to blast Dogger off the face of the earth, what you got to be scared about?"

Edgars said, stammering: "Major Dogger, master, sir . . . He was the man who beat me."

The General stared at him blankly. "You were Dogger's houseboy?"

"Y-yes sir."

"I see."

He stood there staring for a moment, and then jerked his head at Abdul Karan and took him aside, and they whispered together for a while, and at last the General came back and said gently: "You done me a good turn, boy. Maybe you don't know how important you really are, and you know? That's kinda part of the black man's destiny too, the poor sonofabitch never does know how important he is—you know what I'm talking about?"

Edgars shook his head blankly, and the General went on: "You gonna stay with me, Edgars, shine my shoes up for me, real good, and before I kill Dogger, maybe you gonna get the chance to tear his back open with a thorn branch too. You know what historical retribution means? No, I don't figure you do. Now, you go get someone to see about that poor black back of yours. Look for a man named Sergeant Kotru, he's a medic. You tell him I said personally to take good care of you, you understand me?"

"Yes sir, master."

Momentarily, the mocking voice was there again: "Don't you call me master no more, boy." He laughed quickly, and said: "You just call me sir, it's a question of dignity. Your dignity and mine."

"Yes sir."

Abdul Karan was watching him as he went with one of the guards among the trees to where the others were camped, and there was the beginning of a smile on his round, inscrutable face. He turned to the General and said: "It's almost time to change course now, wouldn't you say that?"

The General shook his head. He, too, was smiling, pleased with the way things were going. "Not yet, friend. At twelve o'clock we swing south. And then at six, seven o'clock, I want you, and three of the captains, and eight hundred men, we gonna make us a quick raid, beat the hell out of a place called Kondarugu. You ever heard tell of Kondarugu?"

Abdul Karan was beaming now. "Yes, I was wondering if that thought might occur to you."

"I'm gonna kill me a Prime Minister."

Prime Minister Obote Jendoro, recently returned from Washington and London, had called a meeting of his Council in Kondarugu, the pleasant little spa that lay close by the eighth cataract of the River Dongwe.

The General raised his voice and called: Shine my shoes," and one of the soldiers ran into his tent and came out with a rag, and the General put his foot up on a stone and watched while the soldier rubbed them to an even finer luster.

The General grinned. "That honkey lover's gonna have the Presidential Guard with him, hell, that ain't no more than two, three hundred men. Kinda give us a shot in the arm."

Abdul Karan said softly: "But before you kill him, Guevara . . ."

"Well?"

"We don't know what he was doing in London, do we?"

The General thought about it for a while, and said slowly: "Yeah. Yeah, maybe we should find out about that."

Abdul Karan nodded: "Even when all the fighting's over, when Dogger's dead and gone, when the Kamapan army's been wiped out . . . We don't want a government in exile, do we? Supplied with British arms and ready to move in on us?" He shrugged. "They won't worry too much about Kamapa, but once we take over the diamond fields . . ." He smiled serenely. "The easy way to get the Englishman off his behind and into battle is to threaten his gold, or his oil, or his cotton—or his diamonds. Give me the Prime Minister for a few hours, Guevara."

"All right. You've got yourself a deal." He looked down at his newly polished shoes and said: "The Liberians, do they make good servants?"

"Edgars Jefferson?"

"Yes. Put him on my personal staff." He was laughing again, genuinely amused.

Madame Suande Jendoro, the Prime Minister's attractive young wife, was having tea with the ladies of the other ministers who had been called to the Conference of the Plenipotentiary Tribal Council of Kamapa, while their men wandered in little groups over the grassy verge that led gently down to the river, running fresh and clear here, with the sound of the cataract a distant rumble muted by the heavy vegetation.

The ministers were discussing, not the Prime Minister's recent trip to Europe and America—which had been declared a *casus foederis* and therefore not open for discussion—but the measures which should be taken to quadruple the country's output of cobalt with the use of producer gas or hydrogen, and the effect on the world cobalt market of the new treaties with Belgium, the Netherlands and Sweden.

The ladies had elected to remain indoors, out of the hot sun, in the lovely old stone house that had been built for the Resident of the now-defunct Compagnie Kamapa-

Belge des Hauts Fourneaux; it was now a summer retreat for cabinet ministers. There were peacocks and tame gazelles browsing on its beautiful grounds, among the hibiscus and bougainvillea and brilliant plants of yellow ginger.

Tonight there would be a reception to honor Obote Jendoro, and the ladies were concerning themselves with the arrangements to receive more than a hundred guests. And Madame Jendoro was showing them the new gown that her husband had brought her from London, exciting the envy of all of them.

It was to be a white-tie-and-tails affair, and the servants were busily polishing up the silver and the chinaware that had been brought from Brussels in the Colonial days of the C.K.–B.H.F.

The wind had swung round in the late afternoon, and the breeze that found its way through the ventilation tunnels was hot and dusty now, and Sergeant Roberts had taken over the console while Rudi Vicek slept for the first time in three days.

Bramble, too, was sleeping, flat on his broad back in the entrance to the shelter, catching a cat-nap and waiting for something, anything, to happen.

The sensors were in place, the charts were up to date, and all they could do now was wait.

Sergeant Roberts said: "Edgars, Paul."

Paul moved swiftly to the console, and Bramble sat up and lumbered to his feet, and Paul said: "One way only till we know it's safe."

Roberts threw the switch, and Edgars' voice was low, almost a whisper. He was speaking very quietly: "Two way, Orange, but keep it down."

Paul slipped the silicon silencer over the mouthpiece and said: "Go ahead, Cantaloupe."

"Not much time, Orange, for either of us. I'm with Tiger, he's attacking point eighteen tonight."

Paul said urgently: "Co-ordinates, your own, quick."

"Twenty-three twenty-one, fourteen twelve. He's taking eight hundred men, the remainder on the new bearing, about a hundred and seventy from here, we're joining them after the attack."

The twin red lights on the console were flashing now, the needle on the scope picking up a bleep, and Roberts said quickly: "Get Rudi, someone, quickly."

But Efrem Collas was there, already plugging in the auxiliary, and saying: "It's okay, I can handle it." He turned his back on the others and held the mike close to his mouth and said: "Come in, Skylark, but we're on the air, so stay in range, keep circling," and Paul said: "Hold him there, Efrem, until we're through."

He said: "Cantaloupe, are you safe?"

"Safe enough," Edgars said. "But I can't stay away for long. Do you know who's at point eighteen?"

"Yes, we know, we'll take care of it." Bramble was trying to interrupt, but Paul signaled for silence, and said urgently: "Stay with Tiger, whatever happens. . . ."

The light went out suddenly, and the line was dead as Edgars broke off communication, and Paul picked up the other mike and said: "Skylark? Okay, come in now."

They could hear the plane overhead now, a gentle hum at twelve thousand feet, a trick of the wind.

Moretti said, and there was excitement in his voice: "Tiger's in the open now, crossing the desert and heading south, but they've split into two the main party seems to be wheeling round east a bit, they've got ten or twelve miles to go before they hit cover again."

"How many men in the smaller party?"

"I'd say five, six hundred, maybe more."

"Distance from point fourteen?"

"Fourteen? Ten miles, give or take a couple of hundred yards."

Bramble had come over with the chart, and was marking it, nodding his head approvingly. "Time? Estimated?"

Bramble said swiftly: "Not less than fifteen hours, even if the raid's over in three."

"Dogger?"

"We need twenty-four hours."

"Good." Into the mike again: "Are you packing parachutes?"

"Yes sir, three."

"A night landing, at twenty-three fifteen, thirteen sixteen, what do you think of that."

"Oh Jesus! Hold on, please."

They waited and Bramble said: "My God what's that plane? A Breguet 1050? He'll never land it in the dark."

"Full moon, he should be able to. . . ."

Moretti's voice came over the air again: "Provided you don't mind a busted undercarriage, Orange. Yes, I can do it."

"And take off again with three men aboard?"

Now there was alarm in Moretti's voice: "No sir, positively not; I'd have to put the third man in the tail section and I'd never get off the ground, it's soft sand down there."

"Hold on." Paul studied the large-scale map again and shook his head. "Two men then?"

"Yes sir. Won't be comfortable for them, but two men I can manage."

"What's your fuel?"

"Four hours left. A few minutes more, maybe."

"Pity. Well, never mind, you'll have to land at those co-ordinates as soon as it's dark enough to be safe, let's say nineteen thirty hours, and wait for your passengers—all right?"

The alarm was back there. Moretti hated flying on bone-dry tanks. He said: "How far do I have to take them?"

"You bring them back here, drop them at the landing ground, the finder will be open."

"That gives me eighty minutes to get back to base on seventy-five minutes' fuel." They could hear him sigh. "All right Orange, will do."

"Anything else for me?"

"No, sir."

"If you run out of fuel, try not to make too much noise when you crash; we're fresh out of aspirin. Over and out."

Roberts switched off and looked up at Paul questioning, guessing perhaps what was coming and Paul said: "You're elected, Roberts, part of a two-man army. How'd you like to hold off eight hundred men?"

"Horatio at the Bridge, sir?" Roberts was grinning broadly.

"Something like that." He looked at his watch. "If General Lincoln isn't in too much of a hurry, you'll just have time to get down there and save Kondarugu. You and . . . Efrem Collas."

"Kondarugu?"

"It's just the other side of the forest; you'll have to make a detour past the quicksand, but you know the lay of the land now, it shouldn't be too hard. I'll tell you what you have to do."

He pulled over the map, placed the tip of his finger over the wooded area to the south of the little spa, and gave them his instructions.

The ornate grandfather clock in the hall of the old residency was striking eleven, the chimes of Big Ben, when the first shot sounded.

Madame Suande Jendoro screamed; the shot had crashed through the open window, ripped across the thigh of the elderly man she was dancing with, the Minister for Supplies, spun up from the polished parquet floor in a whining ricochet, and had crashed into the gilded mirror that stood behind the splendid bust of Obote Jendoro that had been cast by the sculptor-poet who had become Kamapa's First Secretary for Foreign Affairs.

The shot was one of many. Out there in the forest that lay across the lawns the machine guns were firing at random, emptying themselves into the house. The Colonel of the Presidential Guard hurled himself at Jendoro and bore him to the ground, covering his body and yelling: "Lights, windows . . . !"

The guests were dropping to the floor, some of the men racing across the crowded room to hustle their own ladies to cover, and there was the sound of iron shutters being slammed as the soldiers outside hurried to close up the windows. The lights went out as someone threw a switch, and all was in darkness.

The machine guns on the roof of the building were chattering savagely, and the officer picked himself up and helped the Prime Minister to his feet and said: "All right, Excellency?"

Jendoro nodded in the darkness, felt the foolishness of the gesture and said: "Suande? Are you there, my dear?" He could hear her sobbing, and he groped for her, and the officer said calmly: "All the shutters are closed, ladies and gentlemen, I think we can afford a candle . . ."

He struck a match, and was pleased to see that the room was suddenly full of his men, and he singled out the Captain and said to him: "What is it, Ensuru?"

The Captain shook his head. "I thought it wiser to come here, sir. Major Filari has the guard under command—whatever it is, they'll soon find out."

"The rest of the house?"

"Well guarded, sir. Whoever they are, they'll never break in."

"Get the ladies down into the cellar. I want you personally, with two squads, to stay at the cellar entrance. Nobody is to break through, you understand? Radio to Sondola for help, the First Battalion."

"Yes, sir."

The Captain turned back to Jendoro. "With your permission, Excellency?" The Prime Minister nodded, and the Colonel raised his voice and called out: "If we could have quiet, please?"

The hubbub died down, and the silence was interspersed with the hard, alarming sound of machine-gun bullets ramming uselessly against the iron shutters.

He said, keeping his voice pleasantly calm: "If the ladies will please all go with Captain Ensuru to the cellars . . . The house is secure. I repeat, the house is secure. The walls are stone, the doors and the windows have been shuttered, and the shutters are all of iron. We all might be a little warm, but the Presidential Guard is in full control of the situation. Now, as quickly and in as orderly a manner as possible, please."

More candles were lit, and the ladies, looking back apprehensively to their men, followed Ensuru out of the

103

room. When they had all gone, Jenoro said to the Colonel: "Well, how correct was that estimate of yours, Colonel? Are we all safe? How long can we hold out here if we have to?"

The Colonel said: "You have my promise, Excellency. If we have to, we can hold out indefinitely."

"And the people in the village?"

"They will have run for the forest at the first shots." He shrugged. "They are accustomed to tribal battles. *Sauve qui peut,* each man for himself. There will be casualties, no doubt. Please God, not too many."

The Prime Minister said gently: "It may not be a tribal affair, Colonel. It just might be that abominable fellow Guevara Lincoln."

The Colonel nodded. "Yes. Or perhaps the even more abominable Major Dogger. They're both within fifty or sixty miles of us." He smiled quickly. "That's why the Presidential Guard is in full force tonight. We have nearly a thousand men here."

In the light of the bright white moon, Sergeant Roberts lay on his belly in the shallows above the cataract, peering down on the gardens of the Residency through the night-glasses.

He watched for a while, and swung the binoculars over to where the machine gunners were lined up on the other side of the river, the tracer bullets clipping through the foliage in red and vicious arcs, and then he got to his feet and slipped quickly among the boulders and swam over to the other side, fighting the violent water, and found Efrem Collas high in the branches of the casuarina tree that hung like a scaffold over the precipice.

He climbed up quickly, lithely, easily among the branches, and whispered: "I make it about five hundred yards downstream, what do you think?"

Collas gestured with his glasses. "No, I don't think so. Take a look at that group by the cluster of palms, four or five men. I'm trying to make out badges of rank."

Roberts trained his glasses on them, and said mildly: "We don't want this to go on for too long, do we?"

"He's goofed," Collas said. "The guards are all over the place. If they've only got two hundred and fifty men, then I'm a goddamn Englishman."

"They're reinforced. We didn't know about it, so I don't suppose the lovely General did either."

Roberts stared at the figures there. "Yes, one of them's a Captain, and there's a field telephone. . . . Will you buy that for their HQ?"

"Depends what you had downstream."

"No, yours is a better bet. Let's get down there."

Collas said: "Hold it, Roberts. It's nice and friendly up here, no patrols, no outposts, no sentries, no nothing. What I call sloppy organization. One unprotected flank, too high to climb, no doubt. But that's useful, isn't it?"

Roberts thought about it for a while. He said at last: "Yes, you've got a point there. I never realized you had any brains, I thought it was just balls. All right then, will you hear me from up here?"

"If you use your barrack-room voice, the one you use for bawling out broads, they'll hear you on Mount Ngaru."

Roberts said pleasantly: "Then that's what I'll do, you Jewish bastard. And tell you what I'll do, I'll make it easy for you. Don't wait for my cue, start firing in . . . oh, five minutes from now exactly."

Collas said: "Christ, a bigot, a white Anglo-Saxon Protestant—how'd you get into this organization? We're all supposed to be bright. And did you bring any of the Colonel's Irish along? No, I thought not. You're a useless sonofabitch, aren't you?"

Roberts was not there any more. He had already dropped in absolute silence to the ground and was making his way through the dense shrubbery down the side of the cataract to the denser forest at the bottom.

The moon was throwing bright beams through the trees, shining back off the water and rippling, and Roberts crawled on his belly to within ten feet of the group of men, listened for a while, and crawled away again, and listened now to the steady rattle of the machine guns. Someone hurled a grenade, and then another, but they both fell short and blew up in the water.

He looked carefully from left to right, forcing his body deeper into the soft forest humus as the bullets whistled over his head, chopping through the leaves with an oddly incisive sound. He thought that there would be maybe three or four hundred of them on either side of him, lined along the bank of the river and waiting for the fire from the opposing bank, where the house was, to come to an end. It would make sense; to keep on firing till the defenders had exhausted their ammunition, and then blast their way across.

He looked at his watch. Five minutes . . .

He heard the sudden blast of fire up there at the head of the cataract, and then he swept his Browning .30 caliber rifle round, set to fire at 350 rpm, and blasted off half a load at the group below him. He was using the modified clip developed by the Private Army's weapons group to hold fifty-five rounds instead of the regular twenty, the bullets of high-impact plastic instead of lead. (This raised the effective range from 500 yards to 720, and the maximum from 3,500 to 5,700.)

He quickly set the cycling rate to 550, and fired another burst, then raced away to his left and fired two more clips. And then he cleared his throat loudly and yelled, at the top of his barrack-room voice: "Major Dogger! Over here! Over here! To me, Major Dogger!"

He heard the sound of Collas' gun still firing up there at the top of the cataract, and noticed that he too was switching from one cycling rate to another, and moving from side to side and back again, changing all the time from ball to tracer to incendiary, an almost unbroken stream of rapid, automatic fire that gave the impression of a large squad of gunners. He heard the bursts of the grenades Collas was lobbing, and when one of them landed dangerously close, he swore and said to himself: Christ, that sonofabitch, he doesn't care about my hernia one bit. . . .

He ran swiftly back to his right, below the bodies of the men there, and yelled again: "Major Dogger, sir! Over here!"

Was he overplaying the hand? He thought perhaps he might be. He switched back to single shot, slipped a clip of incendiary bullets into his BAR, punctured the forest with them in a farewell gesture, and then climbed, silent and unobtrusive once more, back up the steep cliff to where Collas was waiting for him.

He said: "All right, let's go find that aircraft and hitch ourselves a ride."

CHAPTER TEN

BUSANGA HOOK
CO-ORDINATES: 24.01E
13.20S

Cass Fragonard had been waiting a long time, and with great patience, for the chance to talk with her. And now, the chance had come.

She was dressed now just as he had seen her the first time, in nothing, only now there was more of her to see. She was poised on the edge of the river, a naked naiad, her khaki slacks and shirt folded neatly on a rock behind her.

Her limbs were long and smooth and dark, her breasts high and firm, her stomach taut, and he was thinking: That goddam Turk Hamash is around here some place, and I'll bet he's watching her too, wishing he could get down there and bury himself in her. . . . Her long black hair was tumbling down over her shoulders, down to the narrow waist.

For fifteen minutes he had been watching her, watching the edges of the river, too, for any other sign of life; no one was there, no one, not even the elusive Christenson; had the Swede grown tired of his otiose suspicions? Or perhaps they were beginning to trust him now?

After all, he was thinking, half the white adventurers in Africa, lusting for the good old days of *bwana* and bring-my-boots-boy, would align themselves—even if only half-heartedly—with a man like Dogger, who still lived in that long-lost world of privilege. They were a moribund breed, the lost men who still wandered around, like Jonas, half afraid to go home, living on their wits, not really hating the Africans but resentful of them. So why should they distrust him? He was a loner, obviously, and more, another competent gun.

109

He watched her standing there, the hot sun making her naked flesh shine, the shadows of the foliage dappling it fetchingly. And then he looked down into the river and saw the heavy-lidded eyes and the long grey snout, and the corruscations of the predator down below her. . . .

The single crocodile was waiting too, he thought, one crocodile waiting for another, and only one of them was conscious of the other's existence.

When she dived, he stood up quickly and stripped off his shirt, and jumped up into the rock where she had been and watched, and saw the long, ugly snout twitch, and the tail start weaving from side to side as it crawled forward on its stubby prehensile legs, slipping into the water with scarcely a ripple.

He shouted a quick warning and dived in after her, and as she looked towards him in sudden surprise, he yelled: "*En arrière,* behind you!' and swam fast towards her, reaching out.

She turned her head and saw the crocodile, swimming towards her almost lazily, and then his arm was around her waist and cupping her breast, enjoying the soft, resilient feel of it as he pulled her away. Three swift strokes with her and he was at the edge of the river again, pushing her ahead of him, his palms now flat on that ice-cold *derrière* and shoving, and she went tumbling into the grass as he clambered out after her and stood there looking down at her and grinning.

She said coldly: "A shout would have been enough. I can swim, very well."

Her hands were at her loins, September Morn, and he said drily: "I just saved your life, and all you can worry about is I might have seen the color of your pubic hair."

Her voice was frigid. "A shout. It would have been quite enough."

"*C'est vert,* it's green." He switched to French and said: "It's delectable, I like it."

She held his look and said: "If you'd be kind enough to give me my clothes?"

"In time." He sat beside her in the long grass and said:

110

"No one can see us here, but we can't see anyone else either, so we'd better be careful."

"*Eh alors?*" She was suddenly angry.

"We have to talk."

"You have to get me my clothes." She was still covering herself up, but contriving not to be too modest about it.

He said: "My name's Cass Fragonard, and yours is Crocodile."

Her voice was very low, and she stared at him, wondering. "Crocodile?"

He said again: "Cass Fragonard." He tapped his leg with a small stone and said: "*Cassoulet à pieds,* you must have heard of me."

"*Oh mon Dieu!*" There was astonishment in her eyes now. "But . . . *mon Dieu,* what are doing here?"

"I came to get you out." His eyes were roving, peering over the top of the grass. He looked at her body and said: "But if anyone comes, I have good enough reason to be here, don't I? Why do you dye your hair green?"

She said, very clearly, making a point of it: "A *lot* of people find it . . . delectable. But . . . my God! Is the Colonel here?"

"No, not yet. Paul is. And Bramble. A few of the others."

She thought for a while. "But I can't come out now, I'm in position, the best possible position . . ."

"I know that. But you're in very great danger."

"Danger!" There was a sharp edge of scorn in her voice. "He's a fool, Dogger. He'll never find out who I am. As far as he's concerned, I'm a whore, part-time perhaps, but just a whore." She looked at him. "You must have seen them yourself, the lost white women . . ." She was suddenly laughing silently. "Well, almost white, anyway. They wander around the continent with nothing but their cunning and their bodies to keep them alive, a little trading, a little cabaret singing, a little IDB, a little spying, a little whoring. . . . It's a life I know well. It's not insufferable."

"And when he's through with you, he'll kill you."

"Not as long as I satisfy him."

"When the battle starts, you'll be in the way, an encumbrance. And you will have seen too much, learned too much about him. You'll be dangerous. So . . ." He drew a finger across his throat.

She was not in the least alarmed. She had deep-set, angry eyes that easily lost their venom, and the word that came to his mind was *flashing*. Her cheekbones were high, her forehead wide, her shoulders a trifle angular, and he thought he had never seen better breasts in all his life. He cupped one of them with his hand, and then the other, and caressed her down over the taut stomach, and she looked down at herself and said: *"Je suis belle? Tu trouve?"*

He said gravely: "I find you very beautiful." He sighed. "My God, this is one hell of a place and a time to get all het up."

Her sharp nails were scratching at his chest. "You want to make love with me? Now?"

He grinned. "Of course. But I will wait till we have more time. Now . . ." He was straining his ears, waiting for the slightest sound that was not the honest sound of the river and the forest. He said, very low: "There's something you have to do, it's important."

She waited, very alert and expectant, and he said: "When we meet, as we will soon, tell them you've met me before. Tell them we met at . . . Kotoloki, you know where that is?"

"Yes."

"You're sure?"

She flared. "I'm sure, stupid. The village below Mount Ngaru."

Fragonard sighed. "You could find reason to be there?"

"Yes, of course I could. You think I never get off my arse in Mkushu?"

"So tell them you were there six days ago. And tell them that while you were there, I came into the village and suggested that you get out of there, fast, that it was dangerous to stay. That's all you have to make clear to them—that it was dangerous to stay." He thought for a while, and said: "And try to meet me tonight, when there are others present, preferably Dogger himself. And from then on, be ready to pull out at a moment's notice."

He looked at her. Oh, those glorious eyes, those lovely breasts! He said gravely: "Is he treating you very badly?"

She shook her head. "No. A bull, but that's acceptable." She was very calm about it. He looked at her thighs and sighed, and she said tartly: "It's not the first time I've been raped, Monsieur Fragonard, and I don't suppose it will be the last. He is talking now of giving me to some of his men, a favor; they don't see many white women."

"And you find that acceptable too?"

"Less so, but better than getting my throat cut. It's a question of preference, isn't it?"

"Yes, I suppose it is. I'll be on the air to Paul in a few hours; is there anything you want to tell him?"

"Yes, if he doesn't already know, Dogger's headed for the diamond fields."

"And we're going to change his course of direction," Cass said. "We want him on Ngaru. Our own chosen battlefield. I'll get you your clothes now."

He stood up and looked around; there was nothing. He went to the rock and retrieved the pants and shirt, came back and gave them to her, and watched her get into them, and said: "Don't forget, six days ago, in Kotoloki."

She scowled. "I don't forget anything, can't you get that into your thick head?"

"Eh alors. À bientôt."

She did not answer him and he walked away slowly, and almost fell over Hamash when he had gone less than fifty paces. The Turk was laughing silently, and he said: "She's hot for you, old man. But they're drifting back to camp, you'd better get over there."

Cass nodded. "That kind of woman was made for men like me, you know that? Where's the sensor?"

Hamash pointed. "The bamboo by the red and yellow rocks, a purple flower to mark it."

"Bien. I must go now." He grinned and said: "Tonight, I make her a very happy woman, you will see."

He walked slowly back to where the camp was, the three

tents that had been put up for the mess and the little camp-fire where the cooking was done. He stripped his gun down, the FG42 they had given him, wondering if the cycling rate could be pushed up from its normal 600 rpm; this while sitting on a rock and watching the men wander in from their duties.

They were closely confined here, hemmed in by the south-reaching arms of the swamp's crescent, and the bush was alive with teeming Africans, some of them in crude uniforms, all of them carrying rifles. They seemed to spend all their time saluting, and he saw one of the officers, Hendrix, lash out with his foot at a soldier whose salute was not fast enough; the man went down, and Hendrix kicked him in the face and moved on, unconcerned.

The huge *kudu*, that was turning on an improvised spit, fell into the fire, and four of the Africans helped the cook to manhandle it back into position. The sun went down, and the stench from the swamp was appalling, and soon they were all squatting on the ground around the fire, all the officers. Major Dogger sat morose and silent among them. The mosquitoes plagued them viciously as they helped themselves to the food that was carried round.

Someone threw a handful of eucalyptus leaves on the flames to keep the insects away; it didn't do much good.

The meal was nearly over, a silent, distracted sort of meal, when Leila came out of the small tent that was always set aside for Dogger. The major looked around in surprise and then jerked a thumb at some of the others and said: "Now, who don't you know? You met Karnobat, and Manera . . . This is Christenson, and Voskovic, and Ball. And, oh yes, Cass Fragonard, he's new, joined us after you did."

There was a green bandana at her throat, her skirt open, to the waist. The men were eyeing the dark flesh there, and she smiled brightly and said: "Oh yes, I know Cass Fragonard."

The Major looked up in surprise. "You do?"

"Yes, we met about a week ago."

She came forward, her hand outstretched and Cass stood up and took it, and kissed it gallantly. Dogger was watching them, a trace of a frown on his handsome face. He said: "Last week? Where was that, I wonder? Why don't you sit down and join us?" He raised his voice: "Boy! *Tendiri* for the *memsahib!*"

One of the Africans came over with a fresh bottle of *tendiri* and a tin cup and handed them to her, and she said, off-handedly: "Where was it now? Oh yes, Kotoloki. We wanted to re-establish a trading post there, but Monsieur Fragonard convinced me it would be too dangerous. *Santé.*"

She was drinking out of the tin mug, and Dogger said, looking at Cass: "What's dangerous about Kotoloki, Fragonard?"

Cass helped himself to yet another piece of venison, tearing it apart with his hands and longing for some of the good food they served in the Private Army's base, back in England. He shrugged. "Dangerous for a white woman, not for anyone else. The whole area was scared out of its wits, a rampaging band of rebels from over the border, the Angolan border, moving in there. All the villagers knew about it, you know how they find these things out. So they'd all gone, hightailed it for the forests till it all blows over." He grimaced and said: "This meat's tough, it's as bad as Jonas's dumplings. *Pâtes cuites,* he calls them. *Merde!*"

Dogger was frowning darkly, staring at him. "Rebels from *Angola?* Are you sure about that?"

"That's what they said. I checked it out, of course; I wanted to stay too, and wait for Aswani, sell him some diamonds. But the bush telegraph is very reliable when it comes to life and death. Seemed like a bigger outfit than usual, and a very nasty one. I hate overcooked meat."

They were all looking at him now, waiting for the Major to push harder. Karnobat started to speak, but Dogger silenced him and said carefully: "Who is their leader, Fragonard?"

They were all waiting.

Cass shrugged. "No idea, Major. I wasn't intending to hang around too long, so I didn't bother to find out too much. I can't trade in deserted villages, so I came south."

115

"How many of them?"

"Oh, a pretty big force, they said. Five, six thousand of them. Once they get news like that, the villagers don't wait. They go, fast."

"Could it have been a man named Guevara Lincoln?"

"I don't know. Who's he?" He gestured with a lump of overcooked venison in his fist and said: "Wait a minute, I heard about Guevara Lincoln—yes, he's operating in Angola, isn't he? You mean he's crossed the border?"

Dogger got to his feet. "I wish you'd seen fit to tell me this before, Fragonard." He looked at Karnobat. "Give me the map, let's take a look."

The Captain lumbered to his feet and pulled a map out of his hip pocket, and said: "Anything this Frenchman tells you, you can take with a pinch of salt. I wouldn't trust him as far as I could throw him."

Dogger had heard about the fight. He said nothing, but studied the map intently for a few minutes. He said at last: "How long ago was that?"

"Six days. What's today, the seventeenth? Yes, six days."

"And at that time, where was he? Did you learn that?"

"Well, of course, that much . . . They said he was ten days' march away, maybe a little more. Why, is it important?"

"Too damn right it's important."

"Well then, let's see, what else was there?" Cass gazed out into space and thought deeply, and then waited, and the Major said nothing, and Cass said at last: "Well, they were rounding up all the villagers who'd been foolish enough to stay in his line of march, but a lot of the tribesmen are joining him of their own free will." (It was not true at all; the Kamapans were hiding out, fearfully, waiting to see which way the struggle would go; soon, they would begin to take sides, and the dreadful internecine struggle would begin, but not yet.)

Cass went on, reminiscing lazily: "Ah yes, he was going to deploy his troops all over the plain there, that's what really scared them. It always means the same thing, en-

116

forced labor, the looting of the food stores." He said, grinning: "The same kind of thing we do."

Dogger said: "The plain?"

"Yes. The plain below Mount Ngaru."

For a long time, nobody spoke. The Major pulled a protractor from his pocket and took a bearing on the map. He measured the distances carefully, and then looked at Cass and said lightly: "You've got a bonus coming to you, Fragonard. Shall we make it a thousand dollars?"

Cass leaned his elbows back on the soft grass, and looked at Leila and back at the Major. She was sitting there primly, her eyes cast down and her hands in her lap. He was conscious that she had raised her eyes now and was looking at him, but he paid her no more attention and said to the Major, very calmly: "Unless you want to save yourself all that money?"

Dogger stared at him for a moment, and then burst out laughing. He said: "Her? Aren't you a little old, old man?"

Cass said: "Read your Plutonius, Major. *'On n'est jamais trop vieux pour s'arranger.'* You'd be surprised the ideas we get when we're getting old."

Dogger was still laughing. He looked at Leila, cool and distant, and said, mocking: "Well, I told you this might happen, didn't I? I was thinking of poor Karnobat here, but this . . . this might be better. It might make them friends again."

Karnobat was glaring, and the Major said: "Don't worry about it, you're turn will come. How far off are the others?"

Karnobat was gruff, sullen, a hidden fury. "Two miles, at the edge of the swamp."

"All right, let's get over there. We move the guns across tonight."

He stood for a moment, looking at them, and said: "Manera, Zukor, Lederer and Flammer, get on ahead and warn them of the change in plans. I want all the guns, all the men, over the other side by daybreak."

Karnobat grunted. "I don't like it. I like the look of the diamond fields better."

The two Ujpest brothers joined, growling, and one of them said: "I was all set to fill my pockets, Major. I don't know about the others."

Balcovici spat out a thick stream of tobacco juice, and said: "We hit that sonofabitch better if we got our pockets full; we got plenty time, why don't we piss off west, take them diamonds fields first—Lincoln can wait, he ain't going no place. . . ."

Dogger said angrily: "He's heading for Ngaru! You heard him! The tribesmen are flocking to him, he's getting stronger, and that makes sense; he's an outsider, there's no tribal conflict on his own account for him to worry about. We hit him first, the diamond fields after. With Lincoln out of the way there's nothing to stop us."

The young Frenchman from Marseilles, Perrot, was nodding his head eagerly. "He'll be behind us if we go for the diamonds now, he'll be between us and our supplies. The Major's right."

Dogger said contemptuously: "Of course I'm right, take a look over here." He spread the map out on the ground and stubbed at it with his finger as the others gathered round him. He said: "Kotoloki, right here. Behind it, Mount Ngaru. The swamps on one side, the quicksand and the forest on the other." He spread his hands over the southern area and said: "What's the ground like here, Fragonard?"

"A plain, two miles across," Cass said.

"Cover?"

"Big round boulders, like footballs, a hundred thousand of them."

"Good." He looked around at the fire-lit faces. "Guevara Lincoln is a better tactician than I thought he might be. The diamond fields are here, and once we leave them—and we'll be depleted, make no mistake about that, they're not going to give in without a fight—once we leave there, we've got to cross that plain. Now, if Lincoln digs in above us, on Mount Ngaru, he's got us trapped. But he can't get there for four days, maybe more. So between now and then we'll dig ourselves in on the southern slope of Ngaru. Then, when he comes in to set his trap, we'll spring *ours* on *him*. We'll be above him if he wants to fight, and if he wants to run . . . we've got him by the short hairs."

Quietly, unobtrusively, Leila had left her seat by the fire and had gone into the Major's tent. He was throwing a glance there once in a while, but when she came out she was carrying a leather bag, all her possessions, and she crossed over to Cass and sat down beside him, not looking at anyone.

The Major turned his attention back to the map, and said: "By five o'clock in the morning, we should all be across. By six, we can reach the forest. We'd better hide out there for the day and move on at dark, we'll have to haul the guns by hand. . . . Eight or ten hours to Koto-loki, so with a forced march we can make it by daylight again. That gives us . . . yes, twenty-four hours to dig in, it's plenty."

He stood up and took a long deep breath of the night's humid air. "Hendrix, Russo, Ball, and Voskovic, round up the men, get them moving, fast. You find any drunks, shoot them. The rest of you . . . we'll give them an hour to get moving, and then we'll be on our way. Karnobat, you'll be the last across."

He came over to where Leila and Cass were sitting and stood for a moment looking down at them. He said, mocking: "Well, if you think you can do anything with her, old man, you'd better take her out in the bushes now, you've got an hour. You won't get much sleep tonight. And tomorrow, it'll be Karnobat's turn."

In silence Cass rose to his feet. He held out his hand for Leila, and silently they went out from the firelight and into the darkness.

CHAPTER ELEVEN

KONDARUGU
CO-ORDINATES: 23.18E
            13.18S

At the entrance to the palm-frond shelter, Edgars Jefferson was swinging the heavy iron back and forth, the sparks flying from the charcoal in its interior as the wind fanned it to a crackling heat.

Back and forth he swung it, and when the iron was hot enough, he spread out the General's uniform jacket on the flat smooth rock he had trundled into position, spat river water from his mouth in a fine spray over it, and began to press it.

The General was standing with his arms draped over the low branch of a beautiful tamarind tree, his head sunk on his chest, the dejection clear on his face. Beside him, comfortable in a canvas chair, Abdul Karan was checking over the list he had taken from his pocket, a silver pencil poised.

He said: "Three desertions among the young warriors of the Husata tribe during the night. They took their arms with them, one rifle, two Sten guns."

The General did not look up. "Did they take their women with them?"

"Yes, they did."

"Who's their chief?"

"Sankuala."

"Kill him. Promote the first sub-chief in his place."

Abdul Karan made a little note in his delicate, finicky handwriting and went on: "A fight among the Hansupas and the Kawis, four men hurt badly, spear wounds and a bullet wound."

"Take ten men from each of the two tribes, and have them whipped."

121

Another annotation. "Sergeant Brurali complains that Captain Asmalu assaulted his wife. They are both of the same tribe, but their chief is dead."

"Asmalu? Isn't his daughter a virgin?"

"Yes, twelve or thirteen years old."

"Give her to Brurali."

"The Ngoros are angry because they've fewer machine guns than the other tribes."

The General said angrily: "That's your problem, Abdul Karan! I told you, no causes for jealousy among the tribes. How the hell can I hold them together if you favor one over the other?"

Abdul Karan said gently: "You told me, remember, that you didn't entirely trust the Ngoros. . . ."

"I trust them now. Give them Stens and Brownings."

"All right. And that's all for today." He stood up and smiled at the General, and said softly: "I tell you, Guevara, it was *not* a defeat."

The General moved away from his tree and folded his arms across his muscular chest, the highly colored undershirt taut across the bulging muscles. His head was thrown back, his chin thrust out, a Mussolini pose he favored. He said: "A defeat! We went there to wipe out the Presidential Guard, to kill the Prime Minister, and they beat up on us, like we was a bunch of schoolkids!" He said again, savagely: "Hopped up schoolkids, they beat up on us, man!"

"No. We withdrew in good order when we found that an unexpected enemy had appeared on our flanks. It was purely fortuitous, but we learned something we might have had to sacrifice a thousand men to find out."

Guevara Lincoln swung round on him. It was something that had troubled him deeply, the loud voice coming to him out of the darkness, so close by and so completely unexpected. He remembered, with shame, the sudden spasm of fear. . . . Was it fear? Or was it, rather, the access of the knowledge that he was unprepared?

He remembered the shock of it. He had stood there, turned to stone in the heat of the dark jungle, rooted like a mangrove tree, his mouth open and his eyes staring. And by the time he had recovered his composure and pulled the men back hastily—too hastily, perhaps—there was nothing but the solid wall of forest to mock him.

It was that, more than anything else: the *mockery* of it.

He looked at Abdul Karan and said: "Dogger?"

"Yes, Dogger. That knowledge alone is worth a dozen battles. We must have killed a hundred, two hundred of the Guard; our own casualties were far less than that, and the balance was considerably in our favor." There was a sly look of pure delight on his face, the dimples creasing his plump cheeks. He said, raising a finger: "And most important of all, a gift from the ancient forest gods your ancestors worshipped—we found out where Dogger is."

The General swore. "How did he get so far west? Can you tell me that?"

Abdul Karan shrugged. "He's a strong man, he made a forced march, a series of forced marches. But he made a bad mistake, a *very* bad mistake. He should have hit us then, and he chose not to, no doubt because he didn't know just how strong we were, or how strong the Guard might have been. If he had, he'd have walked right over us. But no, he slunk away in the night like a jackal, and left us with one piece of intelligence, of inestimable value."

The General was looking at him now, listening, knowing that Abdul Karan was the best tactician in the whole of Africa. He said: "All right, I'll buy that. We know that Dogger's somehow gotten behind us. How can we put that knowledge to advantage? If we head for the Mwombejhi now, the site you chose so carefully, he'll be right between us and our reserves, the advantages will all be his. He's the one that'll have the room to maneuver. We'll be on the wrong bank, with the swamp behind us . . . just where we planned to put *him*. By day, we'll have the sun in our eyes, and by night. . . ." He was furious, and Abdul Karan smiled, waiting for the venom to run out.

The General was waving his arms now, gesticulating with a clenched fist, and he shouted: "And now he's behind us! Out there somewhere! And where?"

He strode suddenly to the edge of the clearing, and raised his arms to the sky and shouted: "Dogger? Dogger!

You white mother! Where are you!? Come out, Dogger, and fight!"

The Sudanese was waiting patiently. He walked over and took the General by the arm, and said quietly: "And there's another source of information we haven't taken advantage of. Edgars."

The General stared. "Edgars? He's not likely to know very much. A servant. Black trash."

"But *Dogger's* servant. His gunbearer, too. That presupposes a certain affinity between them, beatings or not. For a man like Dogger, a servant, a gunbearer, an African . . . he'd be just a chattel. He wouldn't worry too much about talking in front of him."

The General said sullenly, a touch of masochism: "Edgars will know nothing, nothing at all."

The broad smile was still there. "I don't believe that, Guevara. Another gift from the gods, and we didn't even realize it was there. Are we getting careless? Listen. We can reduce the possibilities to three or four. From here, where will Dogger go?"

"Nowhere. He's out there now, surrounding us, waiting for just the right moment."

"And I don't believe that either; the scouts have found no sign of him. Besides, this is not his kind of terrain, his guns could not be put to their maximum use in the forest. No, he's not here now, he's gone. He's smart enough to know he can't fight us here. But gone where? As I said, three or four probabilities, and we have to reduce those to a single *one*. So . . ."

He took off his glasses and polished them, and said: "He's looking for a fight with us, remember, and he wants to take the diamond fields as well, everyone in the country knows that. The only question is, which comes first? Which one is going to be Dogger's first battle?"

"The fields," the General said promptly. "Those whitey mercenaries always fight better with their pockets filled."

"No. The fields are heavily guarded and he'll have to accept heavy losses, whereas he'll think he can take care of us with almost no casualties at all—except among his Africans, and that won't worry him a bit. No, we must assume that he'll want to fight us first and get the diamonds afterwards; they'll still be there. And he knows exactly where we are now, remember that. It must have come as a shock to him too, to walk right in on our private little fight, but he knows that we're here, and he'll want to figure out where we're going. And there are only three or four places we can reasonably be expected to make for: the Mwombejhi, or Busangà, or the upper reaches of the Dongwe. And maybe, if we could find a way through the swamp, to the plain by the Luena Flats. Now, Dogger is not going to fight on territory he doesn't know, correct?"

The General was listening intently, his eyes narrowed. He thought for a while, and then turned towards his tent and shouted: "Edgars, come over here!"

Edgars put down his iron on the wet moss, the steam from it sizzling, and walked over to where they were talking. He saluted clumsily, and put his heels together, and said: "Sir?"

Abdul Karan said: "Relax, Edgars, relax.... ." and the General said: "The last few days you were with Dogger . . . think hard. Did he send out any scouts to Busanga? Or the Mwombejhi? Or maybe across the Dongwe, up river? Or to Luena?"

Edgars beamed. He still stood stiffly at attention. "Yes sir, General, he sure did."

"Ah. Which one of them? Or all of them?"

"No sir. To Busanga."

Abdul Karan said: "How many scouts, do you remember?"

"Ten men, sir."

"And when was that?"

Edgars frowned. "I don't remember exactly, sir. Ten, maybe twelve days ago. They came back pretty quick, though, and Captain . . . Captain . . . I don't remember his name, one of the captains, he said it wasn't no good, the swamp was too deep."

"I see. And the Mwombejhi?"

"No, sir. I never heard him talk about the Mwombejhi. I don't think I even know where it is. But he sent scouts to

125

Kotoloki, Sir. They came back after three days, and he sent out twenty, thirty more men . . ."

Abdul Karan said sharply: "To Kotoloki?"·

"Yes, sir. I heard him tell this captain that's where he'd go after he finished with the diamond fields; he said the scouts would have the lay of the ground for him by the time he was ready. Ten days he said, or maybe two weeks, and he told the second lot of scouts to wait for him there."

The General frowned. "*After* he'd finished with the diamond fields? Are you sure about that?"

"Yes, sir, I'm good and sure. He said he had to get a lot of loot to keep them white captains happy, so as they'd fight good. Yes, sir, General, I'm sure."

Guevara Lincoln let out a long, deep breath, and looked at Abdul Karan, and the Sudanese said gently: "Yes, even I can be wrong, Guevara. But now . . . now we know, don't we? You see how it all works out for us?" He turned to Edgars, stiff as a ramrod still. "At the village of Kotoloki? The scouts were to wait for him there?"

"Yes sir. No sir."

The General frowned. "What do you mean, yes sir, no sir?"

Edgars squirmed. "What I mean is, he told them to wait for him on Ngaru, that's just a few miles from the village. He said he'd be there soon as he finished with the diamond fields. Ten days, he said, or maybe a few days more."

Abdul Karan said, beaming: "All right, Edgars, go back to your work. You've done very well."

"Yes, sir." Edgars saluted, stumbled as he turned about, and marched himself back to his ironing.

The tension was tight now. Guevara Lincoln said softly: "Ten days or more, we can beat him to it, easy. We can have eight thousand men on that mountain a week before Dogger gets there. You realize what that means?"

Abdul Karan nodded. "I realize it very well, Guevara. He'll march his men to an empty mountain, and it will erupt with an avenging army, and Dogger will be destroyed with all his men. Surprise, the only valid asset in a guerrilla war, the only one."

The General said: "We move out now. Now."

stages that would have been the death of more civilized soldiers. A hundred men with *pangas*, the sharp bush knives of the African, would go on ahead and slash a way through the forest, cutting with speed and an age-old skill, their bare feet trampling a passage underfoot and the knives making the broad trail clear.

Then the others, perhaps a thousand of them, would run at a steady jogging pace for an hour or so, and another hundred men would take the advance guard while the others rested, or ate, or (if they were still carrying bottles from the last raid) simply get drunk while they waited for another mile or two to be cut for them.

They would run on again, their rifles and machine guns slung over their shoulders, the incredibly heavy bags of assorted ammunition on their backs, and in the course of one night they would have covered an impossible twenty, twenty-five, or even thirty miles—through jungle that was considered impregnable.

And in the open, across the dry waterless bush, they would run, without stopping, for as much as fifty miles.

There were eight individual columns now, moving on a roughly parallel course through the forest, over the mountains, across the rivers, up and down the steep valleys, skirting the edge of the swamps, and resting for a few hours at daylight (but no one would see them; it was an instinct to remain well hidden) until their leaders bullied them once more into taking up the trek and getting on with the march.

Now the sun was showing the first streaks of red in the east and Abdul Karan said, wiping the sweat out of his eyes: "An impossible pace, Guevara, they'll never keep it up."

The General laughed. He was a happy man now, an athlete by the side of a fat and flabby man. It made him feel greatly superior.

He said: "You remember the old days, Abdul Karan? The history books? The great King was always the one who could beat any goddamn man that came at him, beat the living hell out of him, off with his head with one stroke of the sword. That's *my* kind of day, friend. I'm the tough-

129

est sonofabitch in this whole goddamn jungle." He grinned. "You've got a paunch on you, man, a paunch like a pregnant broad."

The Sudanese had plumped himself down on a log, and he was panting, his heart beating fast. He tapped his head, and said: "That was a long time ago, now . . . now, it's *this* that counts." He clapped his hands and drank from the canteen his bearer handed him, and wiped the dribble from his lips with the back of his hand, and said: "Thank God for the daylight, we can rest up."

"Yes. We rest here. But we're in good shape now. We make a good run tomorrow night, an easy one the night after, and when Dogger comes in, we'll be waiting for him, man, all rested up and ready to fight. And you know what I like best of all? I like best that he's going for them diamond fields first. You know how they guard them diamond fields? They got machine guns shoulder to shoulder, all the ammunition in the world. They gonna cut him to pieces. Oh, he'll break in, but he's sure going to be cut up."

"His Africans. Not the Europeans."

"Right. That's the way whitey fights: the poor bastard black man out front." He raised his voice: "Edgars!"

Edgars came running, and clicked his heels and saluted, and the General said: "My tent over there, get some men to cut wood. I want it up in about fifteen minutes."

"Yes, sir."

"Start a fire and find some meat. I'm hungry."

"Yes, sir."

Edgars ran off, and two of the chiefs came in and waited for their orders, and the General said: "Pass the word around—I don't want no shooting while we're here. If we need food, they can use arrows or spears, and no fires excepting under the trees. No one goes into the river, no dancing, no noise. We hide here till dark, and then we move on again. Tell them I'll want a conference of the captains an hour before sunset."

One of the chiefs said: "Column Four, General, they found an army patrol and took them prisoner."

"Oh? Any officers?"

"No sir. Fourteen men under a sergeant."

"Then why the hell did they bring them along?"

The chief shrugged eloquently: "Column Four is the Ngoros, General. Savages, they wouldn't know any better. Two of the prisoners have been killed already; if you want to see any of the others . . . ?"

"No. Kill them. Knives, not guns. I don't want no shooting."

"Yes sir."

The chiefs went back to their other men, and a little while later the General was awakened by a piercing scream not far from his tent. He put a towel round his waist, slipped into his shoes, and went to see what the matter was. The Ngoros were killing one of the prisoners by slowly pulling his intestines out of his belly with the help of a Y-shaped twig.

He watched for a while, and said sourly: "Why don't you save that for the white men?"

He went back to his shelter, and fell asleep once more in the arms of the pretty little girl that Abdul Karan had sent to him.

All around the camp the women, the soldiers' wives and the camp followers, were making flat loaves of bread on the thorn-root fires, and pounding millet into flour, and cutting up strips of venison to hang in the sun for drying at the edge of the forest, and washing their men's clothes by pounding them with stones in the creek that flowed in from the river, and spreading them out over bushes to dry.

High in the trees the sentries kept watch. And the rest of the camp was asleep.

CHAPTER TWELVE

MOUNT NGARU
CO-ORDINATES: 22.40E
              12.05S

Now it was all beginning to fall neatly into place.

The time was passing with the relentless insistence of a jungle drum, and the golden slopes of the mountain had become the cyclorama of a gigantic stage.

Major Bramble had wedged himself uncomfortably into the cluster of rocks that had become known as the Crow's Nest. It was a hundred and forty feet above the shelter, on the very summit of the peak, and gave a splendid view of the plain below, the rocks shining with the amber of the dawn now and casting shadows so long that they seemed to reach into that infinity from which the boulders themselves had rolled.

Beyond, the green of the forest was a mantle, still dark, laid over the hot earth, its edges well defined in accordance with what seemed an absolute absence of logic, as though the gods had taken the matted tangle of trees and shrubs and vines and had just tossed it carelessly down, to fall where it might.

On one side was the purple morass of the swamp, its boundaries finite only from up here; and to the other, the deadly quicksands were a startling, blinding yellow.

From this point the whole world stretched out below, alive, vibrant, and somehow . . . expectant; Africa had always known when death was imminent.

A herd of zebra was racing across the plain, a pride of lion in steady pursuit, and Bramble swung the glasses round momentarily to watch the kill. The big male in the lead was fifty yards ahead of the others, and the rest of the pride was moving off to the sides, cutting out a lone straggler. He watched the lion pounce and break the zebra's

133

back with one swipe of a powerful foreleg, and he moved his glasses back to where they had been before.

He said, calling down quietly: "Get Paul, Drima, will you? That plain's getting to be just too damn busy."

Drima extracted himself from the shade of the rocks and slipped down to the shelter, and in a moment Paul was there, the folded chart on a clipboard, his glasses ready.

Bramble said: "Rick Meyers coming in, and believe it or not Aklilu's out there, though you won't see him easily, and over on the left . . ."

Paul said: "I see them. Hamash and Crocodile."

He zoomed the lens of the glasses to maximum, and now he could see the look of savage fury on her face, a lovely, striking face, the flashing eyes that Cass had so admired now filled with anger. Paul grinned; Hamash was walking ahead of her, moving easily among the shadows, and he stopped for her and pointed at the sun, and jerked his head in a motion that meant hurry up.

Paul said quietly, watching: "That damned woman gets up here, she's going to make us all miserable, every one of us."

Bramble said: "Screw her."

"Aklilu? Where?"

"Two points off the acacia trees, a direct line with the first of the yellow boulders."

"I see him. My God, that man can run fast. Could he have seen the others from where he is? Could they have seen him?"

"No. Too many folds in the ground. But it's a good bet that he's seen the dust from Rick's truck—he's heading for better cover, fast."

The legs were pumping down there as the Ethiopian streaked into the copse that lay along the edge of the yellow sand. They saw him emerge a moment later above the foliage, no more than a slight movement in the top of the highest tree, and he was staring out to the west where the truck was. They saw him climb down and continue on his way, not running any more but walking at a very fast pace indeed, and Paul looked at his watch and said: "Eighteen hours." He said to Bramble. "Ten pounds he gets in before Rick does."

"Done. He'll never make it."

"You don't know your Ethiops, a point of honor." He clapped Bramble on the back and returned to the shelter, and the first shadow to fall across the entrance was Aklilu's.

There was no sweat on his gleaming coffee body, and his breath was normal. He said happily: "A bridge across the swamp, just a few inches below the surface, and they took the guns across it during the night."

"Ah!"

"Eleven pieces all told."

"Eleven?" Paul was frowning; the number didn't check.

"Yes, sir. Four Nebelwerfers, four twenty-five pounder gun-howitzers, two 75mm. recoilless guns, and a Bofors 40mm. He manhandled all of them over, ropes and men and nothing else, and they were heading for the forest when I left them. At least seven thousand men, perhaps a lot more, and by now they'll all be well under cover."

"Show me." Paul perched himself on the edge of the flat map rock, and spread the large-scale chart out. Aklilu ran the edge of his thumb across it and said:

"They crossed here, exactly, and were heading for these trees, here, the advance guard lighting small fires already, getting the food in for the main party. Everything carried on their backs, no wheels at all except on the guns."

"Mortars?"

"A lot of them. I counted eighteen in one group of maybe a thousand men."

"Shells for the Bofors?"

Aklilu shook his head: "I looked, but I couldn't find out how they were moving them. But they'd be no problem. Hell, Paul, that Bofors weighs nearly six thousand pounds, and they still got it across the swamp, just man-power alone."

"Y-e-s . . ." He said, musing: "I don't like the Bofors, he's picked up four more guns since we estimated his strength, and that Bofors alone . . . I don't like it a bit."

Aklilu shrugged: "One man can spike it, Paul. He'd

135

have to be a black man, of course, to get in among them."

"Let me think about that. . . ."

The console was playing a tune again, and Vicek said: "Moretti coming in."

Paul said quickly: "Get Major Bramble, Aklilu, on the Crow's Nest," and took the mike from Vicek. He was tense now, and he looked at Vicek and said: "And this is what we're all waiting for. . . ."

Vicek threw the switch. Moretti's voice was excited, and he said: "Skylark calling Orange, in a hurry please."

The excitement was contagious. Paul said: "Go ahead, Skylark."

"He's turned, Orange."

"Good. But remember your drill, please."

The pilot was almost laughing. They could hear the plane clearly now, and Paul dragged the long cable over to the entrance and looked up, and it was there, high up at eight thousand, the sun gleaming on its wings.

Moretti said: "Tiger has changed direction, Orange, he's moving south now, on a bearing of one hundred and seventy-eight, repeat, one hundred and seventy-eight. Seven columns of between nine hundred and twelve hundred men each, out in the open during the night when I couldn't see them, and camped now in the forest out of sight, but their trails are clear, very clear. I got a good look at them just after sun-up, a total of about seven, eight thousand men."

Paul said sharply: "Guns? Any heavy stuff?"

Skylark said cheerfully: "I took a good look, Orange, I couldn't see any. Flew back over the course and found no sign of any wheeled vehicles at all. Just men, a lot of bodies."

"What height were you?"

Moretti chuckled. "I've got all my Cuanza Air Prospecting markings, so I could drop to zero feet. Two hundred feet, Orange."

"Good. I'll want you to activate Hecuba tonight. Stand by, keep in range. I'll call you."

Bramble was there, and Rick Meyers was with him,

covered from head to foot in the fine red dust of the plains, and Paul said briefly: "Tonight. Any changes?"

Bramble shook his head, but Rick said: "Yes, I want Idriss, we've got trouble with the shafts."

"All right, you'll have him."

Ahmed Idriss, the desert Bedouin who had been archery instructor to the sons of the late King of Libya, without a doubt the best living bowman in the world, the only man who could shatter the ancient Turkish records for speed, for distance, and for accuracy. He was resting up now in Algiers after an exhausting reconnaissance of the Afghan mountain fortresses that had nearly cost him his life.

Paul said again: "We'll get him. Poor bastard doesn't have a moment's rest, does he?" He did not question Rick's demand.

He opened up the small scale map and drew his pencil lightly across it as they gathered round him.

He said: "This is Lincoln's line of march, and Dogger's moving on a collision course. Each of them is quite sure that he'll get to the battleground ahead of the other." His eyes were gleaming, his freckled, boyish face flushed. He said: "They're headed, both of them, for the ground we chose. It's going just the way we planned it."

"Are we sure they'll hold their bearings?" It was Rick Meyers, quiet, careful, pedantic.

"Yes. They changed course for the reasons we gave them. If they change their minds again . . . No, I won't work on that assumption.

"All right," Rick shrugged. "Just an idea."

"Can we assume they'll want to get into position during darkness? We'd better decide that right now."

Bramble said: "If they don't they'll make it easier for us, and somehow—I feel they're not about to do that. Dogger, certainly. He won't run the risk of giving away his positions, it's against everything we know about him."

"Rick?"

Rick nodded: "Nighttime, it's what we've assumed all along."

"All right then. Hecuba tonight. Any objections?"

Bramble was smiling. He said: "Tonight. I's beginning to . . . to *tingle* already."

"Rick?"

"Tonight."

"Then that's settled." He said to Vicek: "Get Skylark," and when the lights were flickering again, he took the mike and said: "Hecuba, Skylark. Forty-one, thirteen. Seven-o-five . . . and straight in."

He was still looking at the chart, noting the marks that Drima had made, the colored lines of the twin marches, the red spots that were resting places, the complicated maze of pencil threads that marked the sensors; Betty would be proud of Drima, he was thinking, he knows how to annotate a map. . . .

He said again: "Forty-one, thirteen, seven-o-five," waited for Moretti to repeat the co-ordinate code, and switched off. He turned to Rick and said: "And what's this about trouble with the shafts?"

Rick was holding out a single arrow for his inspection. He said: "That's a Ngoro arrow, and it's the kind we'll have to use, like it or not, because it's the longest shaft used in Lincoln's general area. We need the length for the maximum range, but . . . Well, for God's sake, take a look at it. There's no way in hell of making that shaft fly straight, not the kind of accuracy we're used to. But if we use Odishi arrows, which are better made, we'll have only half the range. The Kasuba shafts are good too, but all the Kasubas are using rifles, and Dogger just might know that, so I didn't want to take the chance of arousing his suspicions. So . . . we'll have to make do with these, and that means the archers have got to have Idriss with them."

"If we straighten them?"

Rick shook his head: "Too dangerous. The Ngoros never fired a straight shaft in their lives; they rely on getting in close, and that's good for us too."

"So we'll leave it to Idriss to handle. After all, we don't need accuracy."

"The one thing we mustn't have, in this case, is excellence."

138

"Good. And Bram . . . you owe me ten pounds."

Major Bramble sighed, and handed over the money.

The sun was directly overhead when Crocodile appeared. Hamash, leading her, was ruefully dabbing at a livid scratch mark on his face, and Crocodile glared at Paul and said:

"So. I didn't believe you'd be here. We've come twenty-five miles in eight hours, and this bastard bloody Turk . . . You owe me a lot of money, Paul Tobin, a great deal of money."

Paul said gently: "Hello, Leila. It's been a long time. You don't know Major Bramble, do you? Leila Tunisia, better known as Crocodile."

Bramble, beginning to beam now and fussing for gallantry, held out his hand, and she stared at it and turned away, and said again: "This bloody bastard Turk . . . He wouldn't let me go back for my diamonds."

"Diamonds?" Paul looked at Hamash, and Hamash grinned and said: "She stole four diamonds from Dogger, and when Cass got her out and handed her over, she'd left them behind. I wouldn't let her go back for them."

She was furious. "He *hit* me!"

Hamash shrugged. The four slashes across his face were deep and scarlet, and he said mildly: "Only once." He grinned and said: "Once was enough, arse over head and a better woman for it. Dogs and women, you've got to teach them not to snap too much."

Her venom was terrible. "Four diamonds as big as walnuts! Thirty, forty thousand pounds worth, and who's going to pay me for them?"

Paul said affably: "All right, we'll give you a chance to get them back, how's that? We'll throw you at Dogger, and anything he has that you can get your hands on . . ."

She was laughing suddenly, all the venom gone, and she put out her hand to Bramble and said: "Well? Don't you shake hands when you meet a lady? Bramble, isn't it?"

He could not contain his surprise, and he took her hand and held it for a long time, trying not to look too blan-

139

tantly at her splendid breasts, the khaki jacket open now and carelessly hanging loose.

He said, stammering: "Would you care for a drink, Miss Tunisia? We have . . . we have some of the Colonel's Irish with us. . . ."

"Irish? Hah! Then Colonel Tobin is here."

"Not yet. He will be. No ice, I'm afraid."

Happy again, he poured her a drink, and she sipped it and looked at Paul and said: "Two things. First, we have to talk. Secondly, do you have water up here? If I don't get cleaned up soon . . . Christ, I can even smell myself; twenty-five miles on foot in this heat, my armpits are cesspools."

Paul sighed. "There's a water hole within a hundred meters of here. . . ."

"Show me."

"All right. Give me two minutes."

He crossed to the console and said to Vicek: "Get the Colonel for me, on scrambler, will you?" He turned back to look at Leila, standing there sipping her Irish and watching him speculatively. Bramble was watching her too, surreptitiously, hoping she wasn't too aware of it, but she turned to him suddenly and opened her jacket wide to show her breasts, and said coldly: "*Eh alors,* take a damn good look."

Bramble turned away, blushing furiously, and gulped his drink, and she laughed and covered up again, letting the folds of the shirt drape naturally from her shoulders. And then the green light came on and changed to twin-red as the scrambler took over, and they heard the Colonel's voice, back there in London and seeming to be right beside them as it came over the main speaker: "Ten seconds for scrambler, hold."

There was a brief silence as the intricate electronics did their work at each end, scrambling all future sound into gibberish to be unraveled here in the shelter and there in the luxury of the Colonel's office-home.

And then cheerfully: "Well, Paul, scrambler's red, so go ahead, how are you all out there?"

Paul said: "Good to hear your voice, Colonel. I've acti-

140

vated Hecuba for tonight, at twenty-two hundred hours."

"Good God, there won't be enough darkness left. You'll have to make it twenty hundred at the latest."

"No sir. Skylark has to make a wide detour to avoid overflights, and he can't fly in daylight either, not with the glider in tow."

There was a little silence. Then: "Does Bramble agree with that?"

"Yes sir. So does Rick."

"All right, then, I won't quarrel with it."

"And I want Idriss, can you get him there in time?"

"Yes, can do. What about Crocodile?"

"She's here now."

"Splendid! Let me talk to her."

Paul smiled and handed Leila the mike. Her voice was low and sweet, an angel now. She said: "Colonel Tobin? I believe we'll be seeing you soon."

He said happily: "Most certainly, my dear, the only reason I'm coming is to see you again. Are you all right?"

She said drily: "Reamed out. But all right."

They heard him clear his throat. "Er . . . not my boys, I hope?"

"Dogger."

"Yes. Yes, I'm afraid that was bound to happen, my dear, once you elected to go along with him. But I'm sure you did the right thing."

"If I hadn't you'd be talking to a corpse now."

"And that wouldn't do at all. Give me Paul again, will you? I'm looking forward to seeing you soon."

Paul took the mike from her and said: "Anything for me, sir?"

The Colonel said: "Cass and Hamash, are they out?"

"Hamash is. Cass still in position. So is Edgars Jefferson."

"But you'll pull them, presumably, before the two sides meet?"

"No sir. They'll get out when they can, under their own steam."

"I don't like that, Paul."

"There's no alternative, sir."

"If anything happens to either of them, you'll answer to me personally. You and Bramble too."

"Yes sir." He looked across at Bramble and grimaced.

The Colonel said: "I'll have to pick up Idriss myself and bring him with me to the staging area, the only way we'll get him in time. I just hope I don't have to search every whorehouse in Algiers to find him. Anything else?"

"No sir."

"All right. Are you taking your mepachrine tablets?"

"Yes sir, of course."

"Good. Over and out."

Paul said gently: "See you soon, Dad."

He turned back to Crocodile. "The pool."

Bramble watched them go, wondering about them as they stepped out of the shelter into the bright, hot sunlight and, constantly watching the horizons down there below them, walked slowly toward the little stretch of deep, cold water, overhung with the heavy green blades of the banana trees and the delicate tracery of a probing, searching vine.

Paul pointed. "There. When you're through, we'll talk."

Leila said: "Oh balls. Sit down, for Christ's sake."

He found a boulder to perch on, and watched her as she slipped out of the pants and shirt and threw them into the water, and stood looking at him for a moment before slipping in herself. She started rubbing her hands all over her body, then found a shallow place to luxuriate in, and jerked her head at the soiled wet mess of her clothes floating darkly on the surface, and said: "Why don't you make yourself useful?"

"I'll find you new ones."

"No. I like my own."

He got up, stepped into the water, and retrieved the clothes and started washing them, and when he felt the hard round inserts stiched in at the beltline, he said gently: "Gold sovereigns? Mad money?"

"None of your bloody business, just wash them."

He sighed. "Maybe I'd better go find some soap."

"Just use a stone to pound them with, we don't have to be immaculate, for Christ's sake, just not stinking so much is all."

She lay on her back in the shallows, letting the water ripple over her long, smooth, brown body, and watched him as he found a heavy round stone and began beating the dirt out of her clothes. Then she said: "All right, where do we begin?"

"First, how many of them are there?"

"Seventy-three whites, the real mercenaries from way back, a bad crowd. But by tonight there'll only be seventy-two."

"Oh?"

"Cass is going to kill one of them, a man named Karnobat. They're supposed to be fighting over me. Karnobat's the expert with the artillery."

"Ah, yes . . ."

"He thought it might be a good idea to kill a couple more of them, but we talked about it and decided he'd better not. Anything to arouse Dogger's suspicions that Cass is not what he pretends to be. . . . You know what I mean?"

"Yes. And after that, is he coming out?"

"Not till the fighting starts. He wants someone on the console waiting for him, in case he can't get back to his last sensor. Now that Hamash is out . . ." She frowned. "That bastard, he hit me!"

Paul said, pounding away: "You probably deserved it. Go on."

"Hamash is out, so Cass has no contact unless he goes back to where the last sensor is. He wasn't sure that he'd be able to do that, or if it would be worthwhile."

"He picked up some more artillery, Dogger. Do you know where he got it? The Bofors, particularly."

"It was being taken to the capital, part of the Zambian Military Assistance Program. It got bogged down somewhere, and Dogger heard about it. He also picked up a couple more British howitzers, the same source."

"Tell me about his officers."

"With Karnobat gone, the man who takes command of the guns is named Voskovic—another bastard. I think he's a Czech. A man called Balcovici, two kids named Ujpest, an American deserter from Korea named Ball—they're the gun experts. Manera, Christenson, Lederer . . ." She rattled off thirty or thirty-five names and said: *"Mon Dieu,* you don't expect me to know all their names, do you? And what good would they do you? *Merde!* If I had tried any harder . . . I didn't want him to suspect that I might be a spy for Guevara Lincoln, unlikely as that might be."

She laughed suddenly, her teeth gleaming. "Maybe not so unlikely at that. After all, I'm not exactly as white as a goddamn daisy, am I? He got a bit suspicious once, Dogger, and asked me if I was a Cape Colored. So I belted him across the mouth, and that took care of *that.*"

Paul held up the clothes and looked at them critically, and said: "I'm not much of a laundryman, am I? What happened when he attacked your trading post?"

"The guns first. Rockets."

"The Nebelwerfers?"

"Yes. Salvos of five at a time. That's a Nebelwerfer, *bien sure.*"

"Yes. What were they loaded with? High explosive or incendiary?"

"Both. He burned us out with them first, and then shelled us. After that, the men just walked in and mopped up."

"The Nebelwerfer was designed primarily for chemical loadings. Does he have any, do you know?"

She shook her head. "I don't know that."

"And do you know how much ammo he's got for the Bofors?"

"Plenty, a team of about a hundred men carrying shells."

"It's the Bofors more than anything else . . . It's a fearsome gun. If we let him use it, he'll wipe Lincoln off the face of the earth before he loses a single man of his own, and I'm not prepared to fight Dogger's seventy-two whites and eight or nine thousand Africans."

"How many men will you have?"

Paul did not answer, and she stood up and said: "Oh

for Christ's sake . . . Fifteen minutes for my clothes to dry out enough to be comfortable—do you want to make love now? I'm clean, more or less."

Paul shook his head gently, looking at the patch of bright green and smiling. He said: "No, not really. I don't like quickies."

"You'll like mine."

He looked at her; she really was a lovely, lovely woman. He shook his head again, not quite knowing why he did. "Let's make it later, Leila."

She was impatient now, her body svelte and smooth, twisted a little away from him, the breasts jutting. She said: "For God's sake . . . Maybe you don't need a woman, but I need a man, so get your goddamn trousers off. Jesus, you're not committing yourself, just fulfilling a need, mine if not yours. A physiological emergency, look at it like that, and do your goddamn boy scout duty. Or shall I take Bramble off your hands for a while?"

He began to laugh and fumbled with his belt, and she lay down on the hot red sand and waited for him.

He said: "Green grow the rushes-o," and wondered if Drima, on guard in the shadows there somewhere and watching for all things, was watching this too.

CHAPTER THIRTEEN

THE UNNAMED PLAIN
CO-ORDINATES: 22.39E
            12.09S

They were all below in the valley now, every one of them except Rudi Vicek, alone at the console in the silent, darkened shelter, with Efrem Collas prowling outside in the black night, a silent, deadly shadow never in one place for more than a moment, and Leila Tunisia left behind to write out her report for the Colonel.

The others were scattered under the umbrella thorns, and Condition Amber was in force now; there was no smoking, no talking, and there were no lights.

The night was as silent as it had been in the primeval days when the mountain had thrust itself up out of the earth; even the animals were silent. And watching, they could see the pinprick luminescence of a thousand eyes, great hordes of hyenas all about them, as though conscious of impending bloodshed and waiting for it, licking their slavering jaws.

Paul Tobin was listening, and Sergeant Roberts tapped his arm in the darkness and said quietly: "There it is now."

Paul said: "Finder on."

The distant hum of the plane was clear now, a long way off, and then the motors cut, and Roberts swung the tiny box around and peered, straining, at the indicator, covering the penlight with a massive, calloused hand, and said softly: "He's cut the engines, bearing one-eighty-three, estimated height seven thousand two hundred, range four point seven kilometers. ETA should be four minutes from now unless he has wind problems."

"Switch on the R-phone, emergency use only."

"R-phone on."

147

The moon was low in the sky, a bank of clouds across it, the pale gleam bright and the Southern Cross shining with a saffron brilliance.

Was it the shape of the glider they could see there above them in the night's silence? Or only their tensed imaginings?

Peering, Roberts said: "He's too high, he's making a pass. Shall I bring him in?"

"Not yet, give him another chance."

It swept over them again, circling, a ghost. They could see the massive wingspan clearly now, and then it was gone from their sight as it glided back over the rim of the valley, impossibly low now. And in a moment it came into sight once more, sweeping over the hill like a seagull, the broad skids less than a dozen feet over their heads.

At the entrance to the tunnel of trees it was no more than a foot off the ground, and they heard it touch down in a gentle *swoosh*. . . . It careened on along the tunnel in the darkness, and they heard the muffled explosions as the wings ejected and settled in the soft sand, and the main body of the fuselage came to a grinding halt among the shadows.

They were running towards it now, all of them, and the doors were thrown off and the men came leaping out in well-drilled silence, taking up their positions, as they had been briefed, along the glider's flanks deep in the shadows of the thorns. Twelve of them, the demolition squad, were already stripping off the long magnesium panels, piling them to one side, unbolting the fuselage swiftly, reducing the massive glider to a pile of long thin sheets; and then Lieutenant Jomo was there—Musa Jomo from Kenya, a lanky, loose-legged young man from the Nandi tribe on the shores of Lake Victoria.

He saluted as Paul came up to him, and took his outstretched hand, and Paul said: "That was a damn fine landing, Jomo. Everything all right?"

The Lieutenant's thin, scarred face was bright with his grin. "Everything all right, Paul. We should have this thing apart in seven minutes; where do we take it?"

Paul Tobin pointed. "There. The forest is less than a

mile, and you'll have to be well inside it. Sergeant Roberts will take your crew there and then lead them up to H.Q. We don't have too much time, and the opposition is probably already moving in, though they're still at a respectable distance, both parties. We've got . . . oh, I'd say three hours to get everyone under cover in the foxholes. . . ."

He was looking around him anxiously, peering into the darkness. "You didn't bring the Colonel?"

"I brought him. Over there."

African eyes, Paul was thinking, the nighttime eyes of a lynx, trained in the darkness of the bush. He stared and could see nothing. He nodded and said to Roberts, close beside him: "Three hours at the outside, Roberts. Keep your sensor open at all times; we may have to guide you through if they move faster than we think they will."

"No sweat, Paul."

He disappeared in the darkness, and Paul went in the direction Jomo had indicated and found the Colonel standing there alone, looking up at the silhouette of the mountain. His face was blackened, as were the faces of all the others, except Jomo. He turned at the slight sound of Paul's feet in the sand, and held out his hand and said: "Mount Ngaru, did you know that the Romans were here once?"

Startled, Paul said: "The Romans?"

"Malthus of Carthage, five hundred years before Christ, a group of his Roman prisoners under Marcus Junius. They escaped and pushed their way south, arming themselves as they went, four hundred men and eighty women. They crossed the Sahara Desert, God knows how, and the whole of the Niger, and Chad and the Cameroons and the Congo, nearly five thousand miles. And they came to Mount Ngaru and were slaughtered, all of them, by the local tribes. How are you, Paul?"

"I'm fine, Dad. How was the glider?"

"It's good. I like it. A pity we have to destroy it."

"We must."

"I know that. I take it everything's ready?"

"Ready. Now it's just the mechanics."

"Bramble?"

"He's getting the men up to HQ and into the foxholes."

"Any movement from the enemy?"

"So far, nothing. I expect the first signs around midnight. It'll be interesting to see who gets here first. You brought Idriss?"

"Yes. And ten archers—are you sure that's enough?"

It was a useless question, and he knew it; it was just good to be talking with his son again.

Paul said: "Enough. All I want to do—and it may not even become necessary—is to give Dogger the impression that an unknown number of Lincoln's men are behind him."

The Colonel said shrewdly: "Then you're assuming that Dogger's going to win this battle?"

Paul nodded. "I think there's no doubt about it at all. He's going to massacre Guevara Lincoln. My only fear is that he's going to be too strong after the encounter, too strong for us to handle. That's why I want a diversion with the bowmen, to move him around if I have to, confuse him a bit, help Lincoln cut him down to a manageable size."

"Did you hear . . . No, I suppose you couldn't have. General Lincoln massacred a Kamapan army post this evening. He killed four hundred and thirty soldiers, cut off the hands of the commanding officer, and sent him with a message to the Prime Minister to the effect that the whole Kamapan army was to be systematically slaughtered unless they came over to him. We've got to stop him, Paul."

"We will. His own arrogance is going to destroy him."

"Edgars Jefferson? Cass Fragonard?"

"Still in position. Each of them turning an army of rebels away from their natural objectives, and putting them where we want them."

"So let's go."

They turned their backs to the breeze and their faces to the purple mountain, walking quickly and silently among the shadows of the empty plain. Below them the long column was winding its way upwards, a hundred and twelve men now, each man carrying his allotted ninety pounds of

150

equipment, some of the heavier boxes, the mortars and machine guns, being dragged on skids with men behind them to wipe out the tracks. Every movement was rehearsed, calculated, unwasted. The demolition squad was lugging the sections of the glider into the forest for destruction. The magnesium alloy sheets, heavily impregnated with sulphate of strontium and an oxolate of sodium to burn with the color of a forest fire, would decompose swiftly and completely, leaving no telltale signs, except ash, to betray its origins.

And when they reached the shelter at last, Vicek was still waiting at the console with a guilty look on his face. Leila Tunisia was smiling as she sipped a glass of the staff Irish in the entrance to the shelter. She was wedged in the opening, her long legs stretched out, her body arched, and she looked like a leopard that had just contentedly gorged itself.

Paul said: "If I find you've left that console, Vicek, for as much as ten seconds, I'll have your guts for a necktie."

Rudi Vicek swallowed hard, and said nothing.

Dogger was already in position.

As soon as the sun had set and the dark had taken over he had driven his men furiously, the captains wielding their sticks over recalcitrant backs, as the Africans sweated over the heavy guns and dragged them across the hard surface of the sand.

For some of them it was easier; there were some who had only to run behind the gun teams, dragging heavy branches to wipe out the tracks. Some of them had discarded their crude uniforms in the heat of the night because of the heavy loads of shells on their backs, and some of them had surreptitiously lightened their loads by dropping their valuable ammunition along the way. (Three men, found doing it, had been killed at once by the captains as a warning to the others.)

Once Dogger had stopped, listening, and had said: "A plane, a long way away, what the hell's he doing out there at night?"

Cass was close beside him in the darkness. "There's a

151

Cuanza prospecting plane in the area; he's been cruising around for weeks now."

"At night?"

Cass shrugged. "So it's a Kamapan Air Force plane; they can't hurt us."

The Major had grunted, and moved on, and in a little while Cass said gently: "Anybody tell you about Karnobat yet?"

Dogger pulled up short. "Karnobat? No. What about him?"

"Look around, Major. He's not with us any more."

The Major stared in the darkness. He reached out and grabbed Cass by the throat and shook him savagely, and said: "What the hell are you trying to tell me, Fragonard?"

The croaking of the frogs in the swamp behind them was appalling, a monstrous cacophony like the roar of heavy traffic.

Cass said clearly: "He stuck a knife under my chin and said to me: 'I'm taking that woman off your hands, Fragonard, give her the taste of a real man,' and she went with him back towards the swamp. It's my guess he's pulling out."

Dogger swore at him angrily. "Pulling out? Karnobat's too good a man to pull a thing like that over a whore, over any woman."

"And he said something about some diamonds. Four diamonds, the size of walnuts."

Dogger ripped the pack off his back and rumaged in it, and could not contain the fury in his voice. He shouted: "Boy!" and when an African came running he said to him: "Get Captain Karnobat. Go find him; don't come back till you get him. If there's a woman with him, bring them both."

As the soldier ran off, the Major shouted after him: "Wait! Better take a few men with you, six men, warriors. I want him brought here. Now." He glowered at Cass and said: "You let him go? I ought to kill you here and now."

Cass shrugged. "He's your second-in-command; I can't afford to fight him with a major battle coming up."

152

Dogger was shaking with anger. He said: "Let's move."

Cass said nothing. He was thinking of the body back there, with Karnobat's own knife driven deep into the side of the neck, a body unbleeding buried under the strychnine bushes, hidden forever except from the hyenas.

They were moving ahead of the others, the main column a little behind them, with Russo, Hendrix, Flammer, and Ball at their head. To their left, two more columns, a thousand men and eight captains to each of them, and further out on the flanks, two more columns on each side, snaking through the night, sometimes closing in on each other, sometimes moving apart as the terrain imposed its exigencies upon them.

They crossed a small stream, the water tumbling brightly over smooth grey pebbles, and Dogger scooped up some water and tasted it and said: "It's good, empty that crappy gypsum water out of the bottles and refill them. We halt for ten minutes, no more."

They were at the brink by the hundreds, filling the bottles and passing them back, and one of the Africans came up in the darkness and said, in Swahili: "Give me your bottles, *bwana*. I fill them for you. Dogger growled and said: "I fill my own bottles, boy, you ought to know that."

Cass felt the tinge of excitement prickling his scalp. He did not turn round at once, but in a moment he looked and saw that it was Aklilu, and he called to him: "Boy! Come here!"

Aklilu walked over to him and stood expectantly, and Cass tossed him his rifle and said: "Carry my gun, I'm getting to be an old, old man."

Aklilu said: "*Ndio, bwana,*" and took the rifle from him and carried it when they moved on, walking correctly three paces behind him. Cass said to Dogger: "Don't count on me to know too much about the lie of the land. I've only been across the plain a couple of times."

The Major grunted. "I don't count on anybody except myself. Don't worry about it, we'll scout it. We've got time."

Cass nodded. "You'd better take a good look at the top of the mountain, Major. If he gets up there . . ."

Dogger said contemptuously: "Don't try to teach me tactics, Fragonard. Anyone gets on the top of that mountain, he's never going to get off it; there's only one route up or down, you told me so yourself. Lincoln's got no goddamn brains; he's a black—but even so, he's not going to put himself into a position he can't retreat from."

"Ah oui, c'est juste."

By four o'clock in the morning, they had occupied the eastern edge of the plain. The guns, eleven of them, were ranged among the huge round boulders, covered over with brushwood and canvas camouflage, and eight thousand men were ranged in battle order in the scrub behind them, squatting motionless under the bushes, hidden among the trees, covered over with creeping yellow vines.

You could have studied the plain intently, and you would have thought that there was nothing there at all. Nothing, that is, except the scattered groups of wandering tribesmen, five or six men to a group, who were walking slowly among the boulders, covering the plain from east to west, searching out the land and studying its tactical possibilities. To the casual observer, they would have been nomads from the desert to the east, looking for water or food or medicinal herbs. You would not particularly have noticed that some of them—the ones who appeared to be the leaders—were lighter skinned than the others; they too were dressed now in rags.

Dogger had sent out his scouts. And one of them, on the southern edge near the forest, was Cass Fragonard.

In the shelter, the Colonel was studying the chart, more complicated now by the maze of fresh lines drawn during the night.

Drima said, pointing them out one by one: "They passed these sensors here, numbers 18 to 23, 71, 79, and 111, at one o'clock in the morning. 48 picked them up, the same column by the looks of it, at two thirty-five, so the column might be anything from seven to twelve hundred men. We've tried to estimate their speed, but it won't be constant, of course. Two hundred and three, and all sensors to the west of it, are silent. So they haven't moved past that line."

The Colonel nodded, and Paul said: "All that presupposes they're in position along the eastern edge of the plain. There's a lot of cover down there, so I'm sure we won't see a single one of them."

"All right," the Colonel said, "let's take a look. Can we use the Crow's Nest?"

Bamble shook his head. "No sir, it's on the skyline. But there's a lookout point to the east of it, thirty yards below it. Same field of view and far less chance of being spotted."

The Colonel crossed to where Leila was sleeping, flat on her back on the sandy floor of the shelter, and he touched her lightly on the shoulder. She was instantly awake and sitting up, and he said quietly: "We have to be very careful now. I'd like you to come along with us."

She nodded and followed them outside, crouching down in the shadows of the rocks, slipping among the banana trees to where the sand-and-sage canvas had been stretched out over a foxhole and covered over with scrub, a slit left to see through.

They wormed their way into it and studied the land below them, and Paul said, his voice a zephyr of a sound: "Bearing one-three-eight, five men, one of them's a white man. One-eight-seven, four more, another white man. Bearing one-twenty—is that a gun there?—directly below the boulder with the obsidian on its face."

Bramble was staring intently. "Could be. That brushwood wasn't there yesterday. Over to the right a little, two more suspicious bushes that have appeared from nowhere."

"I've got them. Chart."

Bramble took the glasses from his eyes and handed over the clipboard, and Paul carefully marked the positions and went back to his binoculars again.

The Colonel passed his glasses over to Leila and said: "Four groups of nomads wandering across the plain. See if there's anyone there you know."

She took them and they waited, and she said at last: "One of them is a man called Hendrix, and I think an-

155

other is one of the Ujpest brothers, the older one. What are they looking for?"

The Colonel shrugged. "As little as a fold in the ground. Anything that can hide an enemy."

"And yet, they're all keeping to the plain. Nobody's coming up this way."

Paul said: "They might. If they do, we're ready for them. One patrol missing, or coming in late. But this place is a deathtrap, neither side is going to use it. That's why we chose to."

She said suddenly: "Cass Fragonard!"

"Where?"

"By the forest, halfway along," and Bramble said gently: "Bearing one-six-nine exactly."

Cass was walking like a tracker searching for spoor, his arms resting on the rifle across his shoulders, his eyes on the ground, and there were three Africans following him, looking at the forest to their left; they seemed uneasy about it, and one of them pointed to where a column of dark smoke had left its residue in the motionless air. They saw Cass shake his head.

Paul said: "There's still smoke left from the fire of the glider. A forest fire, it happens all the time, no problem." He was watching Cass's group carefully, and he said at last: "And Aklilu's with him, they've made contact. Good."

Bramble was still searching for more guns, trying to locate them by the brushwood camouflage, and he said: "Six of them, for sure, but I can't see which are which. The Bofors would almost certainly be somewhere in the center. . . ."

Paul interrupted him: "We don't have to worry about the Bofors any more."

"If Aklilu doesn't get to it."

"All right. Then the Nebelwerfers will be on the flanks, I'd say, and the howitzers on either side of them. But that's only a guess."

The Colonel said: "Your battle, Paul. But I suggest you'll have to have the men for the guns mobile. They'll